# Listen To Your Skin

## An Anthology Of Queer & Self-Love

Eds. Stina French & Folauhola ("Evey") Vakauta

LISTEN to your skin PRESS

First edition
ISBN: 979-8-218-37226-2

Cover art by Hannah Ross-Smith
Cover design by Folauhola Vakauta
Interior layout by Folauhola Vakauta
Edited and proofread by Stina French

Printed in the USA

Listen To Your Skin Press
Denver, CO
listentoyourskinopenmic@gmail.com

Dedications

For anyone who has ever been told they are too much, too loud, too sexual. And for my mother, who deserved more pleasure and less pain in her too-short life than she got.

-Stina

For the people who show up.

-Folauhola ("Evey")

# Contents

# The Origin Of Listening To Our Skin

Stina & Evey

*"if i open my hand to you/like this/palm up and out,/do you see a request or an offering?"*
*—ellie swensson, "Open,"* Salt Of Us

Evey & Stina:

The works in this compilation come from participants of the Listen To Your Skin Reading Series, aka "literary sex church," which began in January of 2021 and has continued since then on the last Sunday of the month via Zoom. People attend from all over the country, and sometimes other countries. Below, we talk a bit about what the event means to us, and how it all got started.

Evey (co-host/Zoom tech):

I was still working at Enterprise when word of a quarantine began to circle. The murmurs grew louder as COVID-19 locked down Wuhan, made its way to Washington, and New York City shut down its schools. School systems and businesses nationwide followed suit. Stina moved all her classes online, and the kids brought laptops home, as remote learning became the new norm.

I remember being upset that I and my coworkers had not been ordered home yet, spending another few weeks cleaning cars, wondering if someone flying in for their mountain vacation might bring complications. Because we had been late to the shutdown party, the door to the house my immunocompromised partners were in took no compromise in shutting out the global pandemic and me along with it. I took shelter with my roommates, whose employers asked them to keep up production while I was laid off and learned to sew fabric, carve spoons.

Our first time grocery shopping was hectic, unsure if we needed gloves with our masks or how long we might be on lockdown. With everyone in a rush to stock up on toilet paper and canned foods, the only people moving slowly that day were the workers. The world stood still, watching, wondering when we might be allowed to hold our loved ones again. Eager to stay in touch, we were online broadcasting our everyday happenings, baking banana bread, dancing, making music, sharing memes, pain, and anxiety.

Naturally, the poets made rooms. In an effort to stay connected outside of six-feet-apart neighborhood strolls, Stina would send Zoom links to poetry events and other literary gatherings. The access to readings I would otherwise never witness was a luxury I did not know I needed, a space we have since taken for granted. When we were finally able to moderately integrate our lives, we would spend Wednesday nights with The Ugly Mug based in Orange County, Friday nights with Nomadic Press in Oakland, or attend a weekend performance with professionals like Gayle Danley, Jericho Brown, Ross Gay, or Andrea Gibson. The reach of these rooms to lives around the country was previously experienced only at yearly conferences like AWP (Association of Writers & Writing Programs), or local events, if you were lucky enough to be near a scene.

Stina (host/founder):

My "Cassandra" friend tried to tell us it was coming. We didn't want to hear it and went to AWP's annual conference for writers and teachers of writing in early 2020 anyway, a way Evey and I loved to travel together once a year, exploring a new city. Me going to panels and writing manically all day, newly a practicing and publishing writer myself and finally *in it*, the swing of it, having my own favorite authors and themes to follow. Evey would go exploring out in the world beyond the convention center with their cameras. We'd meet up at night and eat delicious local food; I'd share some snippets I'd written and they'd show me their photos. That year was San Antonio, and I have no idea how many tacos we ate, but it was a lot. My back had been acting up, so they made a bed in the back of the car and drove the whole way.

We went because it was a hard thing to let go of, even with the indisputable medical facts. The conference was sparsely attended; almost all my favorite authors had decided not to go. We finally admitted we shouldn't have, either. In May of 2020, the *New York Times* published "US Deaths Near 100,000, An Incalculable Loss." The 2021 death toll (~415,000) surpassed the 2020 numbers (~385,000). At the time of us writing this foreword, over one million Americans have died in the global Covid pandemic. The divorce rate experienced a 95%-136% increase, by the best estimates, driven largely by women-identified folks. Capitalism ground on, and my own minor personal tragedies progressed as well. My girlfriend and I, both immunocompromised, were especially afraid to catch the virus. She predicted the end of everything: her job, our relationship. She, too, was Cassandra-like in this. Her amped depression and withdrawal and my amped anxiety and insecure attachment led us into a slide from which we never recovered. The lack of access to Evey, due to their work situation at first, and then their roommate's exposures later, didn't help. I have never grieved a relationship so hard in my life. It was actually kind of impressive how much I cried and for how long.

I wasn't sure I cared to live anymore, but I still cared for art, so I indulged that, at least. I'd started writing a book, and I kept at it, inspired by the events we were attending. I read on the open mics and in the workshops with Dorothy Allison in the room, Ani DiFranco, Brendan Constantine, Tara Hardy, and they listened kindly, and they listened deeply. Some of them even private-chatted me to tell me how much they had enjoyed my delivery. I felt so *seen*. The validation was heady like a drug. It was all I lived for during this time.

Eventually, I led an erotic writing workshop as I began to edge toward my sexuality again. I tried to help participants do what I was trying to do: tune into my desire and pleasure. We wrote and we laughed and we cried, and no one wanted to leave when it was over. We wondered if there were any way we could gather and share on this deep level again. I thought, my god, yes, why not? I mean, I've attended more online literary events in the last year than anyone I know, and I think I throw a pretty good party. And so, Listen To Your Skin was born. I asked two of my favorite Denver-local writers if they'd be willing to feature for the first one on the theme of "self-sex," which surely everyone was having more of during the pandemic if they were having it at all. They said yes and delivered such amazing sets we were blown away. For the next month, I had the eggs to invite national and international slam poetry champion, Gayle Danley, to feature. She also said yes and delivered a set that included going topless and inviting the audience to do so, as well.

I knew we had something here.

Evey:

She always said she started Listen To Your Skin as a way to mend a broken heart. The months of watching her get back into her body, attuning again to her own desire, finding self inside self, was inspiring. Covid had a lot of folks questioning and restructuring their lives and relationships. With so many of our friends picking themselves back up after heartbreak, it came as no surprise that everyone wanted to talk about and process what they had been going through.

What we found was not something new, just something that we've grown away from because of the work hustle, the life hustle, that keeps us separate from our communities. It's with others that we find the strength to heal and grow, in sharing not just our pains and frustrations, but also our joys and successes. The space created when we come together is holy; the collaborative allowance of showing up for each other is divine.

I have watched our participants grow in this space, become more vulnerable and comfortable in themselves as they pay careful attention to each other. To facilitate this space is such a great honor and privilege, makes me feel like a raised garden bed.

Stina:

I have watched Evey grow in our space. It took them a whole year and a half to speak on the open mic, and then it was only because I signed their name on the sign-up sheet without permission. The one they'd patiently edited each month, others' names on it, never their own, always willing to hold others' bags and baggage, and yet never quite exposing their own aching, tender innards. I watched as they finally let themself come up and out and cry a little, take up space. They read a piece about their mother and religious trauma and the cruelty of SCOTUS and being one of 11 children. They talked about dividing chiclets gum to share and said, "We don't make space by subdividing." I watched the sea of faces in the Zoom room resonate with their words, quote them in the chat.

When I think of how encouraging our participants have been of each other, I swell with pride. I am often guilty of bragging about it, the supportive atmosphere, but also the high quality of the work being read.

Evey:

I have witnessed and been a part of many gatherings but have not found any spaces that hold reverence quite like Stina holds for this event every last Sunday of the month. The ability to hold a frame for difficult conversations where all parties *feel* heard and *are* heard is a talent that more event hosts could do with learning.

Ceramic artist Paul Briggs says, "A pot without a community is just an empty vessel." The idea of this container began as a call-in, an offering to bear witness, an arcing bridge between grief and love. It's a lot to hold, an abundance. We had a bout of nerves before our first official event, and really, before each event after. Hosting requires grounding. We began a ritual of dropping in together just before we went on-screen, touching noses, sharing a deep, slow breath. We remind ourselves that the space is not about us, but about everyone who shows up, and then we open the room.

Stina & Evey:

Listen To Your Skin is a space for the people who show up, who share what they might not be able to elsewhere, their tenderest pieces. It's a space to experiment and explore the self, become more of who we are, to heal, and feel held and received in this. This vessel offers horizons, spills when necessary. It is an open prayer for understanding and communion.

We hope we've conveyed some of the magic that is our little gathering, and where we've failed, we trust the pieces that follow will fill in the rest. We invite you to join us some last Sunday to listen and to write, to witness and be witnessed.

We are reaching out our hands, offering this book to you, dear reader, these raw, vulnerable, sometimes steamy, sometimes sad, expressions. This is an offering, to be sure, but also a request. What we want *most*, as you read, after you read, maybe when you're writing later, inspired by what you find here... What we want most is that you keep listening to your skin, and then, please, oh *please*, come and tell us what it told you.

# A Poem To Make Your Mom Want To Be A Trans Faggot

Andy Izenson

I'm not a home wrecker in the sense that I'm going to sleep with your husband
although I might sleep with your husband. What I mean is that if nobody ever told you before
then let me be the one to tell you: if you think you can't be good enough
at being a woman to make it stop hurting, you're right.
I know you're afraid and I can't tell you not to be
I know you have bedtimes, hard times, bloodless knuckles,
rules and safeties piled teetering on the toy soldier of your re-solve,
a hundred hands grasping for the familiar shape of you and I wonder
if you've been wide-eyed at five in the hungry morning, holding so still to keep the overfull cup of your want from spilling out into sobs,
if you've dragged your thoughts like a desperate dog away from the eternal escape hatch of
maybe my car will just maybe somebody will just maybe this airplane maybe this ex maybe—
if you've got something hidden at the bottom of the sock drawer of your spirit that you only let yourself look at once a month—

if you've been wishing for something you could pray to for an earthquake—
Look, I don't know what angel of ego death took my hand and told me I was allowed.
You put these land mines here yourself. Nobody needs to show you the door. Your world has been warping to circle towards it a little more every day. There's no key anyone can hand you
but here we are, you—hungry for newness in a way that you can only understand
as the desire to be fucked—and me, symbolizing nothing but myself,
ready to love what you're hatching yourself into with my whole heart and then
dissipate into a memory of pleasure.
You haven't breathed this air before so if you're light-headed,
if you're hungry, if it aches,
step forward slowly,
step back slowly,
you're going to have to relearn how to dance.

# Kid

## Kel Hardy

"Another one?" Hal asks, shaking their tall-boy at me.

I hesitate, then nod. They retreat to the kitchen and I exhale into their skyline view. What am I doing here?

Hal is Ella's wife. Ella is my friend-sometimes-submissive. When Ella and I first met, I assumed Hal would join us at some point, but I was quickly corrected.

"Hal only likes femmes," Ella told me. It seemed like a binary way of looking at it, but I shrugged it off. Hal was small-town and old-school and it wasn't my job to educate them on internalized heteronormativity. However, every time I got in a room with them, I was like a freshman at the seniors' table. I laughed loud, told too many jokes, and picked my nails while they looked around the room at anything that wasn't me. I wanted to impress them so much it felt physically painful, so I began to avoid them. But then Ella invited me over for drinks, and I arrived to find only Hal and a six-pack.

"Ella wants us to make nice," they said.

For two awkward hours, we made small talk. We talked about basketball, the city, Hal's work, my lack thereof, and, of course, Ella.

"How did you two meet?" I asked early on, grasping for commonality.

"She walked up to me and my buddies playing darts and said she would go home with whoever hit a bull's eye," Hal said.

"She didn't realize I wasn't a guy until I won."

"So you were her … first?" I asked.

"Yeah," Hal said. "That's why we ended up opening up. I didn't want her to feel like she missed out on anything."

They chased their confession with a sip of beer. My heart swelled at the beauty of their sentiment. We returned to less important topics.

Now Hal returns from the kitchen and silently offers me a glass of amber liquid. I catch a whiff of caramel and smoke.

"Whiskey?" I ask.

"Out of beer," they reply.

I watch them sit down through my tipsy haze. The light from the kitchen casts dramatic shadows over their sharp jaw and clean crew cut.

"Why does Ella think we need to make nice?" I ask. Beer makes me bold.

Hal takes a slow sip and stares at their own glass.

"Well, I wasn't sure you liked me all that much, and she wanted to remedy that."

"Me not like you?" I say, too loud and incredulous. "I thought you thought I was just some stupid kid fucking your wife."

"You are some stupid kid fucking my wife," Hal says. They roll their head back against the chair to look at me. In the dark, their eyes are all black.

"Hal," I say. "I do like you. I just felt like I was just this snot-nosed embarrassment, so I steered clear."

"Maybe you are an embarrassment," Hal says. "Maybe you like it. Maybe I do, too."

I feel a rush surge up in my body. This was not what I expected. Hal looks down at their whiskey swirling in their glass.

"If I told you," Hal says, "that I want to embarrass you more, how would you feel?"

My mouth is dry and I'm already breathing heavy. It's alarming and humiliating how ready I am. I nod frantically.

"Good," Hal says. "Stand up."

I'm a marionette, and their words are strings. I stand in front of them, feeling my eyes widen like a puppy dog.

"Jacket off," they command.

Marionette, strings. I shiver in the evening air. I look down at my body; my nipples are hard through my sports bra. Hal stands and steps closer to me. They survey me like they're assessing my worth. I feel small. They run their hand up my hip to my chest, gently brushing over my nipples. My mouth draws open as they lean in; I could cry from wanting.

They pinch my nipple and twist. I yelp.

"Shut up, kid," Hal hisses in my ear. "I've got neighbours."

I whimper softly in their ear and nod. I can't remember the last time I bottomed, and I had never craved humiliation. But here I am, buckling at the knees, turned on by my own pain and the promise of more.

"Take off your fucking pants," Hal growls at me.

I scramble at my buckle, suddenly losing all coordination. Hal grabs my shoulders, spins me around and thrusts me against the banister.

"I can't trust you to do anything right, huh kid?" Hal says, reaching around me to unbuckle my belt. "I hope you're better when you fuck my wife."

They pull my belt off with a quick fluid motion, so my loose jeans fall to just above my knees. They yank my boxers down too.

"Are you ready, boy?" they growl in my ear. I turn my head towards them, craning my lips upward. They grab my face in their hand.

"I'm not going to kiss you," they growl. "Not yet."

They shove me forward so I double over the railing then back away. I stay bent over with no instruction, goosebumps rising on my bare ass and thighs. I feel the leather of my own belt running over my ass, and I brace myself. I know exactly what's coming because it's exactly what I would do.

*THWACK!* My belt cracks against me. *THWACK!* So much for the neighbours not hearing us. *THWACK!* I screw up my eyes against tears.

"You like that?" Hal asks. I nod silently. I hear them step to the side, and feel their knuckle run down my wet cheek. They bring their fingers to my lips, and I suck greedily.

"I think we should wait and talk to Ella before we take this any further," Hal says. I cry out a wordless objection, feeling my insides crumple and my brain struggle with language. I need them now. They press their lips to my hair to shush me, pulling up my pants.

"Soon, I promise," Hal murmurs. "For now, come sit in my lap. I'll give you a kiss."

# Mechanical Test of the Gag (or She Fag)

Ahja Fox

1. I suck ink out of pens because

    A. batteries
    B. locker dials
    C. screws, a librarian's glasses

2. It tastes like

    A. zipper
    B. another body bag
    C. alcoholism (w/o bottles)
    D. my hair in cherry knots, tops off rainbow brite dolls

3. Adhesive limbs

    A. my thighs learning the shape of her face
    B. her face learning the shape of my thighs
    C. my thighs, her face—the shape of ophidian tongues
    splitting book spines

4. Rainbows are birds unhinged from the blue

A. it's true, I was standing under a rainbow when a single wing clipped my left hip after a girl kissed me there
B. it's true, two years later, they half-mooned over the same girl's body hidden behind kaleidoscopic parasols, the day ending with thesmashing of their beaks on her casket

5. I can use a speaker diaphragm as

A. a cereal bowl
B. a piss bowl

6. If the dust cap is missing it is because

A. I swallowed it
B. I used it to plug a blood bath that would drown all the children in Sunday school

7. Death

A. hangs from eyelashes
B. dangles like fringe off shoulders
C. recites every poem written into the bodies of paper cranes

8. Her name

A. a tree
B. half covered in frayed ribbons
C. reaching for my throat flush in white
D. pages … from a tea-stained bible

9. The gag (the she fag)

A. a puckering slit
B. an itty-bitty slot
C. the transmuting pink that follows rather than fills

# I Call Myself an Atheist, but...

Kit Tara Eret

I call myself an atheist, but...

I'm not sure where the idea came from—perhaps I wanted a symbol for my budding kink explorations—but I ordered a necklace of Kurukulla online. She's a dakini, a female spirit, dancing on the body of Rahu, devourer of Light, shooting magnetizing arrows that attract auspicious events. Originally it would take her a week—the following Friday—to get to me, so the tracking bot said, then Wednesday, then Wednesday but with the apology that it was running late; then it arrived on Tuesday, like she couldn't wait to get to me.

I call myself an atheist, but...

The top I'd been playing with cancelled on me, said she's double-booked. The beating I so wanted wouldn't happen. I felt despondent and abandoned till Kurukulla told me to reconnect with the secular community. So I go to the Secular Hub, a place I hadn't been to since the Before Times, before I'd transitioned. Nerves jangled as I walked through the doors. Will they all shriek in horror at my femme presentation? No. Friends greeted me openly and warmly and invited me to their social table. There I met Summer, a man who expounded on his trials and tribulations, how he lost his dearest friend to AIDS, being in and out of hospitals and drug rehab and homelessness. How he felt inspired by his trans friends to slough off his old identity and go by his drag-queen name. Currently unemployed, with a medical condition that could kill him, he was one of the happiest fuckers I'd ever met, delivering a sermon on egolessness that I needed to hear.

I call myself an atheist, but...

Kurukulla showed me an event that piqued my interest. A sex party at a tantric temple. I vacillated. Fear of the unknown and cultural shame at my slutty desire ate at me. But Kurukulla had other plans: she guided my fingers over the keyboard to RSVP and pay for the ticket. I thought of backing out several times, but was also elated. I drove through the city, watched couples leave their cars happy and expectant for carnal adventure later that night. I wasn't any different. The temple was an unassuming house among many on the block. The hostess greeted me in a fishnet jumpsuit, clearly showing her nipples and pussy. Such transparent sexuality was refreshing! I, the atheist, grasped the Kurukulla pendant for support. I entered the house, surrounded by its erotic and psychedelic mood. Posters of Eastern deities hung on the walls and colorful projections danced on the ceiling. In the room I sat down in, porn quietly played on a TV in the corner while people engaged in pleasant conversation about ghosts and spirituality and higher meanings in the mundane. Some smoked pot, its smell tickling my nose. Two women began playing, rubbing each other's pussies. I liked watching and I wanted more, but was afraid to ask to participate. I went upstairs where most of the action was happening, figured I'd just masturbate and leave. Instead, three guys surrounded me, ready to play. I liked the attention. After quick introductions and consent to play, they fondled my breasts and pinched my nipples to pleasure-pain. I sat back in a chair. One guy got down on his knees and fondled my cunt. It didn't matter that she still looks like a cock. The other two, I sucked their dicks. Kurukulla flowed in me, through me, my shame gone, my orgasm peaking, washing over me. I felt free. I stayed a while longer, lounging in a chair and lazily masturbating as I watched other scenes, coming down pleasurably from my erotic buzz.

Leaving the tantric temple, I turned, bowed in reverence, and again clasped the Kurukulla pendant. But, you know, I'm an atheist and don't believe in that shit.

# I've Never Done Anything so Meta as Writing Poems for a Reading Series Called "Listen to Your Skin" While Sitting on a Nude Beach in Europe

Kona Morris

The first time I came here, I didn't know what it was
Just wanted to explore the island, try to find a less crowded beach
See how far the walking path would take me

There is a sign, but I didn't know what it meant
Two happy breaching dolphins and the letters "F. K. K."
Three letters my American eyes had never seen strung together before

A grove of trees
A bend in the path

And I am transported into a curious new reality—
Whole families, free from all articles of clothing

Floppy dicked grandfathers, standing proudly in the sunshine
While golden-skinned grandchildren play in pebbles at their feet

Lovers laying together
Sisters and brothers climbing onto paddle boards
Mothers and aunties making lunch

There is no sense of shame or pride or strange
All body shapes and sizes
Equally seen, but none noticed

Some with pelvic hair
Some with bright red rashes, covering the cheeks of their asses
All in the open air

And it's not just at the beach
Both sides of the walkway and everywhere in between
Families are camping
Hikers hiking
Children biking

Grandmothers with tits that stretch across sagging bellies taking naps under a tree
A giant man with his tiny shriveled foreskin
A lady with slender breasts, rolling slowly in a wheelchair

There is even a bar in the F. K. K.
Where friends sit, on bare ballsacks and labia
Sipping pivo and playing cards

The F stands for "Frei," as in *Free*
Körper is Corporal, *Body*

Kultur is *Culture*
(And don't you love how English is German)

*Frei-Körper Kultur!*
And they really are.

It is my favorite beach here for many reasons
Least crowded, calmest water
Closest to where trees outnumber signs of civilization

Though, I don't know that I could be here with my family
Stand to see my father or brother
My mother with my son

Maybe I'm too brainwashed by the chains of cloth I grew up seeing
Maybe I am not that free

But, alone, I am one of them
Alone, these are my people
The Free Body Culture
Under the sun and in the sea

Sitting here, I am both hidden and protected
As anonymous as I am naked

And there is nothing I've experienced in this life more spectacular
Than feeling the sun shine into my shyest of cracks
And the way my breasts perk
As I'm sliding naked through the sea

# Tasting Notes

HanaLena Fennel

I want to be a taste that gives up its secrets
easily.
I want to burnt sugar and cardamom this body;
tip and pour as sweet aromatics and leave a mark,
iron bound and oak stay-put.
Call me the black label burn
dressed up on the edge of the table.
Crave the tinder of my tongue.
I'm not here for your posturing smooth choke lie.
This is a *Smoke me if you got me, boy* kind-of-night.

I want to hold your tremble in my incisors,
push past the tense doorway of skin,
swim in your body until it feels feral and saved.
To swallow the low moan of yes
escaping the sides of your bit lip,
pull us both into the deep-wanting-well of me
and believe this water is the good stuff.
I want to hurt you and have you say thank you.
To tear at your veins;
make pomegranate jewels,
bloom them on your surface,
and gift back sacrifice as
sacrament.

# An Exploration of Plated Passions

Aida Manduley

***Avocados: yielding***
you split and slide open, giving options
(concave and convex and complex)
to consume you,
exposing gaps for me to fill
with a tentative probe and hot mouth.
your buttery brightness melts on my tongue,
subtle and smooth,
like the curves encased in tight green skin
give way to my fingers,
yielding to pressure and pleasure,
turning creamy with more churning,
offering a dark pit as keepsake.

***Mushrooms: wild***
i send my hands to dig under rotted wood
for fungal fruit, meaty and wanton,
eyes peeled for fleshy black trumpets
and fruity chanterelles so golden yellow
i forget the sun.
there's a thin line between speaking in tongues
and licking my lips, asking for more,
like an indigo milk cap at knife-point,
bleeding blue to match your eyes.

adventurous, i crunch on forest-fire burnt soil,
bags full of collected morels
that make the most of tragedy, and smile.

***Oysters: slippery***
i want you to give me salty tangled lips i can kiss,
creaking open like secret shell doors
to expose insides soft and ready,
lips that smile at siren-songs
and shore up the weight of my wetness.
i want you to sing me things of the sea,
where brackish water whirlpools a tune
and you slide freely, humming against my cheek,
sinking deeper into some sort of dream.
i don't want furtive glances and tentative touch;
just diving headfirst slip-gliding down fast
back-scratching and drowning.

***Grapes: divine***
i'm entranced by your tongue-tied divinity–
body weather-worn and textured,
skin whispering stories of sorcery
as timeless as a broken watch.
clumsy clustered thoughts and midnight kisses
collected in a goblet for resurrection,
plump memories fit for crownless kings
and the serpentine sirens who love them.
my hidden places i've revealed willingly,
upturned stones and rabbit-holes,
pockets emptied
for your holy ghost to enter me.

***Honey: sticky***
this joy is not like brimming over with wonder,
sunlight bursting from my belly in hot, crystalline shards–
sharp, bright, and violent.
this joy is liquid trapped in my stomach, thick and viscous,

slowly seeping, creeping, crawling up my throat
and spilling from my mouth.
it's a weighted happiness, enveloping and consuming,
covering from the inside out, sticking to bones and skin.
its waves sink me down into soil until i'm buried,
cocooned in dirt and the paths i've tread,
body breaking down and decomposing borderlines
until i am boundless too.

***Ginger: stimulating***
in a mind with no memory,
everything is sensation and present tense,
past pains and old lovers gone with a flutter of lids.
in a mind with no memory,
all's a wonder with no unraveling,
just reveling in electric currents
running lightning fast and silent, burning into bones,
fingers splitting skin until
everyone sees the suns and roots beneath.
this is a body reduced to its nervous system:
not tangled, but entwined, tentacular and probing,
only feeling, not recalling.

***Figs: bruised***
instead of sewing leaves to cover sin,
peel smooth skin to reveal
the unexpected pink of a jawless fish;

a fissured fig with teeth blossoming,
the funnel-mouth sucking sucking sucking.
frightening folk tales aside, just close your eyes
and let the luscious meat roll in your mouth
before the purple slit shows it overripe and ready
to burst in a blaze of glory.
yes, lawrence, ripe figs don't keep,
but there is always wood, always seed, always womb
from which more can come.

***Chiles: hot***
my body can withstand the burning
of time and temptation,
scorched earth erotica testing the limits
of my passion and patience.
my skin can cradle bright bellies full of fire,
melt off my bones and slip back on like a robe.
my wardrum heart can beat slick and sweaty
pumping blood and fists in protest,
cheeks smeared with the charred bones of history.
but give me a tongue-tip heat test
and my eyes water, the buds burn:
this is my only weakness.

***Beets: bloody***
tongues and teeth slick with sin
keep secrets like caged harpies,
mouths bursting with song and seed,
lips pigmented red like an unblossomed bruise.
with color scraped from wombs and roses,
the rich red trail downward sloping
is an uncoiling spiraled snake
from a venus mound turned flytrap.

taken in reverse, copper pennies turn sweet,
salty tang turns the earth-taste of primal war-paint
splattered and channeled
into cupped hands overflowing.

***Chocolate: dark***

in my country, liana lullabies
swing at night, wrapping loosened limbs
in dreams of you, but
one pound of god-fruit is all i'd need
to really reach your distant shores.
in looking for heartstring currency,
the tropical trees heard my call:
fruit pods cracked open like eggshells,
spilling debris from swirling stars
in dark yolk currents, bitter spice,
swallowed whole,
by your black-hole mouth.

# When the Prince Rescued Her

## Rachel Ann Harding

When the prince found her, she was safely in the tree. After he coaxed her down, he "saved" her from every other man by cocking her down. She knew it was going to happen. If her mother hadn't told her, her stepmother had told her; the old woman had told her—this is what happens. But she was not his victim. She was not ruined or made a conquest. She did not want him, but sometimes things happen that you do not want, so she simply turned away to take in the love of the moss cradling her knees. She let him move in and out, but felt only the forest breeze caressing her lips and labia, flowing in when he pulled out. He was nothing but the sensation between the forest fucking her and that is what she wanted. When he was finished, she did not take his hand to help her up but grasped the branches of the willing fir tree that left sweet-smelling sap on the flesh of her palm.

They began the journey to his castle and when they stopped for the evening, she let the river water, cold as the stones, wash away his stinking heat from all parts of her body. He was a necessity, like a chair or an amusing bear at a festival, but he would not be in her story for long. Her eventual destination was a cottage deep in the woods where lavender and nightshade twisted together. But first, there were the children to bring into the world, with her lover the forest and their surrogate father, the prince. Oh, he was handsome, he was smart enough, had enough, but he was not and would never be enough for her, for she had loved the bare limbs of the trees in winter and counted the stars beyond the fireflies; she had lain with the dew as the badgers howled their lust and had found release over and over to the moon rise curled up with the roots of the oak. The prince could not compete with her lover the forest, and thankfully, he was not smart enough to realize that.

# Prove Me Right, Prove Me Wrong

Kiki DeLovely

I have a thing for assumptions. Secretly, I love them. You may think it strange that I get an erotic charge off others taking liberties, but just hear me out. There's a certain quality of bold bordering on brazen, a confidence edging right up against cockiness that I find so damn sexy. Not to mention the self-assuredness it takes to not only trust your intuition but to actively pursue it. When someone follows their gut instinct with a level of respect, playfulness, and desire for enthusiastic consent, it really gets me going. Whereas most people detest others assuming certain notions about them, I revel in either proving them right or proving them wrong. I suppose the proof is in the pudding … so to speak.

The moment they first sat down across from me, I felt an intense spark of attraction. A long table full of folks and I could feel their gaze on me. Luckily, I was working on a project that I could busy myself with, only occasionally looking up to steal a flirty glance. Gorgeously genderqueer, a sexy shaved head and beautiful brown skin a couple shades darker than mine, Tasio took one look at me and decided to ask me something in Spanish. Their first assumption. One I adored proving right. I answered shyly, briefly, barely able to meet their gaze. Then they were called away. And I was filled with dread over an opportunity missed.

My disappointment melted away easily, however. Kink camp was nothing if not filled with endless possibilities.

"Come with me." Taking me brusquely by the arm, my friend practically dragged me across the dining hall, whispering, "You're gonna want to see my newest crush." He had assumed correctly. As I followed his gaze from a safe distance, I was equally enraptured by just how handsome she was as I was by what he had to say about her. "Wicked smart, good politics, and a hard-hitting player."

"Mmmmm ... Yes, please." Zero shame in my voyeuristic stare, nor the fact that I was practically drooling.

All it took was that one moment and I had appropriated my friend's crush. Divine intuition or a presumption, call it what you will, but I knew simply by looking at her: Janus was soon to become my lover. What I didn't know was the extent of her staying power—both in the bedroom and in my life.

"Well, well, well ... look what we have here." Speculating that it would make me nervous as hell, my supposed friend brought Janus into the kitchen later that night. "She looks even tastier than whatever smells so damn good coming out of that oven." The pair double-teamed me verbally, making me blush hard and harder with their teasing and raunchy remarks.

"And I bet she smells delicious, too." Janus's greedy gaze roamed audaciously up and down my body, poring over the lacing of my corset, taking in every last frill of my petticoat. "Had I known this is where they hide the snacks, I would've gotten here much earlier."

Barely able to breathe, let alone form any intelligible response, I was squirming with discomfort as they circled me like a pair of sharks who enjoyed toying with their midnight snack as much as they did devouring it. I'll confess: I loved every moment of it. They flustered me to such an extent that despite my chocolate pudding cake already being in the oven, I had to search out other imagined tasks just to give myself something to do other than flush and flounder under their shameless overtures.

Taking pity on me at last, they took their leave of me, but not before Janus gave me my first command. "Come find me later on."

Never one to disobey and ever the unconventional flirter, a couple hours later, I plopped myself down on the barn bleachers directly in front of Janus, assuming she wouldn't mind me casting the spotlight of my attention in her direction. She was fucking her partner, and I took the opportunity to make my flirtations clear by designating them as my own personal form of entertainment. And good goddess, was it ever entertaining. There were all kinds of elaborate scenes happening all around us, but voyeuristically inserting myself into their scene was far more captivating. Janus started running commentary, flirting back with me as she fisted her boy ferociously, all the while her boy eating up every second of this kinky coquetry.

Just when I thought that my panties couldn't get any wetter and I began to fret that the fuck fest might pass without me getting any actual action, an assumption was my saving grace.

"You." The confidence in their voice rose above the surrounding cacophony, commanding my attention.

Like a fool, I glanced at the empty bleachers around me. Certainly they couldn't be pointing at me? I had been so ridiculously bashful around Tasio all weekend. But apparently that didn't deter them. They beckoned me from across the barn with one outstretched finger that sent my clit reeling. Before I realized how I had arrived beside them, Tasio was cutting to the chase.

"You like fisting." Coming from their lips, it was more an undeniable statement than a question, so I just smiled. "Giving or receiving?"

"Yes, please," was about all I could utter, paired with a healthy dash of eyelash batting. Their direct nature and my palpable attraction to them left me a mumbling mess. Luckily, they were making this easy for me.

Tasio grinned. "I thought so." Apparently, they had a thing for assumptions as well. "I'm starting a daisy chain and I'd like you to be the one to fist me."

I had never heard the term "daisy chain," but I wasn't about to admit that. I wanted to prove myself worthy. So I followed them over to a small crowd of hot queers, quickly catching on as they explained who would be fisting whom. Janus, never one to be left out of something she wanted, had finished with her scene and swiftly declared that she would be the caboose of this train. And that she would be the one fisting me. Rendered completely speechless—*what sex goddess had graced me with such blessings to be positioned between her and them?!*—I simply reached up under my skirt and pulled off my panties, handing them to her as a sign of consent.

Janus smirked. "Red. How apropos." She accepted my offering by stuffing them half-way into her rear left pocket. Assuming her rightful position as omega—while energetically she was nothing short of alpha—she lived up to her divine namesake. The rest of us fell in line, getting down on all fours, and the daisy chain consisting of no fewer than six of us quickly took shape. We all agreed on the collective safe words, donned latex gloves, and diligently lubed up our fisting hands, wherein I discovered that Tasio was a lefty. A helpful bit of information that I tucked away in my memory for future use. My healthy side dish of optimism shining through.

I worked a couple fingers into Tasio just as Janus was working hers into me, which, as you might imagine, was beyond distracting. I found it nearly impossible to keep my attention dedicated to the task at hand (*ahem*) when suffering such intense pleasure. Between all the libidinous buildup and the thrill of the unknown, Janus really hadn't any actual need for lube, but once she got going, I was certainly grateful for its presence, unrelenting as she was.

While I was busy trying to not be too assumptive with Tasio, making my way slowly into their front hole, Janus decided to take a stab at a couple assumptions she had of me. Going from three fingers to all five in the blink of an eye, she plunged her entire fist inside me in one fell swoop. "I had a feeling you could take it, you little harlot." Taunting me lecherously. "Your cunt was just begging for it. She just swallowed me up like she's been starving for weeks." Proving her right about both my accommodating nature and my love of dirty talk was quite the prideful pleasure all my own. However, her tone dripped with satisfaction at her presumptions being spot-on.

I recall glancing up for the briefest moment—a second that stood still in time was all the distraction I could afford—and noticing a highly appreciative audience gathering around us, respectful to give us space, but clearly reveling in their own garden of voyeuristic delights. I had a fleeting vision in my mind's eye of how provocative we looked from above—writhing on the mats below, each body beginning before another ended, churning like a well-oiled machine, fucking in time to an unheard beat, the music of our cries rhythm enough—and then was immediately sucked back into the scene, the supreme somatic nature of our activities slamming me into my body as I squirted all over Janus' wrist, her boots, and the mat below. Janus groaned with gratification, "If you're lucky, I'll make you clean that up later, dirty girl. I do love a good tongue against my leather."

These words spurred my desire all the more, and I couldn't help but fuck Tasio faster with three and then four fingers as I continued to impale myself on Janus' hand. Struck by the haptic intensity of it all, I felt very much in my body while also playing a part in a more powerful network. The kinetic energy bursting forth from Janus then raged through me, continuing its pulse into Tasio, and undoubtedly repeated the fervent favor as the chain snaked on in front of me. A view quite titillating to take in—I could only catch glimpses of faces but the variety of shapes, colors, and textures of all the asses was more than sufficient eye candy. Let alone the scent. The heady redolence of lust permeated the air, all of our earthly pleasures mingling into an olfactory orgy. My nostrils flared and my lips parted, inhaling the petrichoric musk through my nose and mouth, I could taste the pheromones wafting down the back of my throat. Someone somewhere up ahead growled with a low rumble like thunder, the gravel in their voice reverberating within me. Together, we all fell into grace.

Taking great care to open Tasio up gradually, slowing to add my thumb, I did my best to ease the thick of my hand into their hole at their instruction. When I was met with greater resistance, I backed off and fucked them in and out with just my fingers, stretching them wider with each thrust. "Ohhhhh, fuck yes!" Pushing back against me hard, Tasio finally allowed me full access with a shriek that enthralled our growing audience. Janus twisted her fist inside me, working my G-spot tenaciously, making me elicit a few shrieks of my own as I squirted again. No matter that we weren't a closed circuit, the energy of our daisy chain was clearly circling back around, surging with gaining momentum through each of our bodies, fueling the fuck.

"What a dirty little whore you are for opening up to me so quickly." Janus made all kinds of assumptions as her dirty talk grew dirtier. "Not that I mind. I enjoy pushing sluts to their breaking points. Especially pretty ones. Pretty ones who provide gorgeous views...." She lifted my already short skirt a bit higher and kept up a steady stream of explicit expressions the entire time. "And watching you spurt all over my boots? That's a vision burned into my brain that I'll be relishing for some time to come." Janus oscillated between threats of not letting me lap it up later and *really* showing me a good hurting if I didn't take it, all the while thrusting her fist in and out of my cunt. I'll tell you, small hands may make for an easy fit, but in no way did she take it easy on me—fucking me with a ferocity that made me cry out until my vocal cords were rendered raw and all but aphonic. I both feared and fantasized about what pain the full strength of those hands could inflict.

A fantasy I couldn't entertain for long as I felt Tasio begin to clench around my hand calling out, "Just like that! Don't move! Oh, fuuuuuuck...." Once, twice, three times, I let them fuck my fist at their own rhythm, nearly crushing my knuckles with the power of their orgasm. Riding the waves of pain and pleasure, I found myself coming again while Tasio eased off my wrist slowly. Janus sadistically pulled out of me with one final thrust, leaving me gasping and quaking, challenging me not to subject Tasio to the same malicious motion. Slapping each of my ass cheeks for good measure, Janus left her mark on me before discarding her glove and bringing the trash bin around for others to do the same. Then she stopped at me.

Looking up at her, unsure of what exactly she was scrutinizing, Janus just stood there with her head cocked, leering over me. "How is it that your lipstick is always so perfect? Everything else about you looks like you've been thoroughly fucked. Nothing short of utterly disheveled. Everything except your lips."

I beamed back with my flawlessly crimsoned lips, proud to have bemused her. "It doesn't come off. At least not without some serious make-up remover and a little elbow grease."

Janus took that as a challenge and reached down, grabbing me by a fistful of hair before bringing me to her mouth. I had assumed that she would be equally good with her tongue as she was with her hands and she did not disappoint. Neither did my lipstick.

When we parted, I saw a spark in her eye as she gazed in wonder at my lips. A new challenge lit her up from within.

"I'll find another way." And thus began Janus's year-long obsession with ridding me of every last speck of my kiss-proof lipstick. A tale for another day involving oil-based chapstick, much scheming, and a massive cock. But I will tell you this: her assumption was spot-on and I enjoyed every second of her proving me wrong.

# To Receive

## Duffy DeMarco

The first time
I left your home
with bruises
I knew
I would be returning.

The second time
I became reacquainted
with my own alchemy
my ability to transform
searing pain
through heat and breath
into ecstasy.

Next time
there was heavy wood
brought swiftly across my ass
and I counted loudly
all the way
to eleven.
Exclamations of gratitude
at each exploding smack
of contact—
giving thanks loudly for

being beaten
thoroughly

out of my element
Taken willingly
where I had been
seeking to visit
but so far
had not found
my way to
alone.

Now
filled and stretched
beyond expectations
I claw my way across the mattress
twisted into unnatural
shapes
bitten
wounded
overtaken
like an animal
in chase

I will not pull away
I endure
I submit
I sustain.
I will take
all of it.

Give me more
please.

Even as my tears
climb their way
to the exit—
even in utter collapse
I am over-coming

my defiance
shines red and bright
where the delivery landed
Tiny ruptures
of fresh blood
making its way
to air
if only for a moment
rising up
in contrast.
My war medals
glistening.
I'm collecting them.
Every one.
I haven't found my limit
yet.

So
you find the limit
for me.

There's always an end.

Even if I forget.
Even if I get lost
and thrown sideways.
There is always

a portal
with secured and guaranteed
entry to sweet rescue
and relief.

You come
gently now
You've shape-shifted.
You blanket me.
Pull me back
through my tongue
with dark chocolate
and reassurance
coveted praise.

In this comfort,
I feel myself
returning.

Naked
exposed
unfinished
in your lap
my cheek pressed firmly
against the fur of your
soft belly
you gaze down
to make eye contact.
I am seen
but I am still
so far down
beneath

I draw ladders
from your eyes
I use them
to climb
as I refill
all that was
ceremoniously
emptied.

Rewarded
with sweet honey
bear embraces
I curl myself small
into that expanse
pushing up against
and through it.
Unfurling finally
in the wholeness
of my own skin.

I have come
back to my myself
after this valiant quest
carrying
a secret spell
I keep forgetting:

How to let myself
receive.

# I Can't Turn Off

Karen G

*What turns me on (Masseduction)*
*I hold you like a weapon (Mass destruction)*
*I don't turn off what turns me on*
*Smilin' nihilist met*
*Angry glass half full*
*Drinkin' Manic Panic*
*Singin' Boatman's Call*
*Teenage, Christian virgins*
*Holdin' out their tongues*
*Paranoid secretions*
*Fallin' on basement rugs*
*—St. Vincent*

I was maybe always meant to be
slutty

I grew up in a town with 12 denominations
in a square mile
*Teenage, Christian virgins*
*Holdin' out their tongues*
was our MO
in an 80s that fetishised
looking at asses in Jordache jeans.

I smoked pilfered cigarettes
and became
a serial lover
I was that girl who had one prom date
and wound up watching the sun
come up from the backseat
of another's car.

Now I'm
attracted to freckles and a little bit of meanness
my friends call me
chaotic good top
after-care specialist
energy
the best hugger

or something.

Despite gross things that happened to me on ferris wheels
hotel & dorm room floors & bunks
and in the back seats
of blue Chevettes

I like wrestling with other bodies
fucking around and finding out
grabbing, pulling, yanking
causing friction
(but not biting).

I will gum and drool on a solid shoulder
sunkissed with freckles
that's my kink

along with a dykey queer appreciation
of hands.

Deshaming and validating
is another kink

My love and my lust
know one thing
—if the kiss doesn't work
nothing else will!

I've tried to get around
the bases
of being base
tried to be nerdy and theoretical and academia
book-knowledged
tried forcing intellectual attraction
into a priority over
chemical reactions, juvenile giggles
over sugar-in-my-bowl euphemisms
—and it works about as well
as a misfiled
card catalog.

Musty, dusty love
couldn't be educated
into making the tongue kiss right.

I'm that punk-gendered mess of a queer
who loves riding buses and metro cars for the bumps and the squeals
who loves being tossed in uncontained flight turbulence
(it does something for my Delta)

the transsness of transportation
corporeal, a body remembers the wrestling matches
the pillow fights
the mouths and hands who met it
from roller coaster make outs
the under-boardwalk salty explorations
the places where parts fit together and jostled awkwardly in
fumble
felt the next day.

I am raunchy
and my love is weirded by the way it leaks out
over the edges of boxes
*I can't turn off what turns me on*
I like to be on top, bottom, side
over under, sideways down
twisty and in control and thrusty
whole mouth, whole palm whole hand.

I am a whole body
of long fingers I inherited
from an ancestry
of wild women.

Is it weird? I don't know
*"I can't turn off what turns me on*
*I hold bodies like weapons"*
even my own.

# Ambisexual Forearms

Valentine Sylvester

The outer demeanor, furred, tan, emerging from a dapper, rolled-up white oxford shirt cuff, casually forceful, the hard curve from working out, on arm day you can barely lift your phone afterward. Slivered to a neat, tapered wrist at the beginning of a smooth, commanding hand, square palm, insinuating knuckles. Slim, short fingers like the pods of a plant, succulent. The inner arm with her map of Prussian veins, the wide tiger stripes of parallel scars from oven burns in the hot, steamy clank of the kitchen where you palmed the line cook's mons in the pantry.

I belong to you. I'm your most devious tool. A cock you can display in public. When you see eyes land on my fur, on my chipped porcelain smoothness, eyes landing with curiosity and trembling on the wide angle between delicate wrist and firm thumb. A top always has the suggestion of an erection in her hand. When you absently move that thumb with its irascible double joint, thighs sigh apart. I'm a limb that you don't have to imagine. I am solid. I can wrap around the ask of a bare clavicle. I can open and slap. I can protrude my digits and slide them like a tongue.

# When Goddess Forgets

## D. L. Cordero

Leather bustier, fishnet pantyhose, a dolled-up mannequin held a paddle and smiled at Ava from within the display windows of Sultry Sensations. She stood staring, palms clammy, fingers tingling. She could've bought it online, but she wanted to feel the soft nylon, stretch the spandex, make sure she could maneuver the velcro straps. Making her profile on SameGenderLovingLadies.com gave her fever. Now she needed the right hardware to sweat it out with the woman of her choice.

She stepped into the warmly lit shop and greeted the bright-eyed salesclerk. Beyond cushions, toys, and lubricants, on a wall filled with glorious harnesses, The Joque, with built in o-ring, commanded Ava's attention. She reached for the shining fabric. God, she was gonna look good in red.

Then it happened. Again.

Yellow store lights flickered like candle wicks against wind. Ava's foggy breath billowed until every sight, sound, and sensation disappeared. Three seconds, five. The previous blackout lasted fifteen. Ava was up to twenty seconds, thirty. The dark around her took on texture. Jelly-like, warm, and wrapping around her.

Walls, shelves, floors reappeared; overhead lights strobed on. Ava clutched the harness so tightly her nails dug through the spandex and into her palm. She shoved down screams. No more six-hundred-dollar ambulance rides to shrinks who'd find nothing wrong with her. She wiped her face, then turned toward the checkout counter.

She met the heated gaze of a young woman. Flawless deep brown skin. Lips the color of carnations. Her dark eyes, like midnight and mystery, made Ava restless.

"Hola, mistress."

"Who?" She blinked.

"You'll take me home, too."

"Baby, I could be your momma." Ava tried to push past. "Tryna tell me what to do."

The woman's long lashes flicked down. She leaned forward. "No one tells mistress what to do." She stroked the red spandex in Ava's hand. "But I have what mistress wants most."

Ava slapped that girl's face, but that child grinned, and Ava felt a thrill bloom inside her chest, petals scattering into electricity that radiated through her body.

"Um, is everything okay?"

Ava snapped her attention to the salesclerk. She whirled to the register, swiped her debit card, and hustled to the door. When the woman didn't follow, Ava hurried home.

She set her shopping bag on her polished coffee table. Striding across hardwood floors, she grabbed a bottle of whiskey and dropped into her living room couch. Peering through the bay window overlooking Lake Merritt, Ava mused over the uninterrupted view of downtown Oakland. High-rises silhouetted by waning orange light. She kicked her heels onto the coffee table and poured herself a shot.

Sunlight flickered. Air grew cold.

"Shit!"

The baffling dark rushed her like an inky hand, smashed her into the couch cushions. The blackouts had never come this close together.

"All I want is some good freaky sneaky before you take me, Lord!"

The membranic texture of the distorted space reminded her of a spoon chasing jello, pressing, digging, scooping. Her tumbler shattered against the hardwood floor when the sunset beyond the bay window glowed again. Ava's fingers shook, malty aroma wafting. There was a sharp knock at the front door.

"Aw hell nah."

More knocking.

"Not today, Satan."

"Ava?"

She straightened up. That sounded like her neighbor Steve.

"I'm dropping off the keys so you can look in on Godiva." A pause. "Thought I heard her come in," Steve said to himself.

Her cellphone rang. Ava frowned. There was no way whoever was out there didn't hear it going off. She backed into the bookshelves by the bay window and clicked the green button.

"Hello?"

"Ava? You ok?"

"Uh huh." *Fuck you, Steve.*

"Um, we said we would meet at six thirty."

"I forgot. Leave the keys there, Stevie. I'm in my house coat and bonnet."

Rustling. Tap of metal on wood. Steve's keys hung on a lanyard. He must've looped it around the doorknob. "Money's on the counter, Ava. I'll be back Tuesday."

Flip flops slapped against the hallway floor.

Never had the idea of babysitting an overfed cat been more stressful. Ava grabbed the whiskey and drank until her head felt fuzzy.

Thirty minutes later, she stood with her ear pressed to the front door. Deep breath. Nothing and no one through the peephole.

Ava knocked over a broom as she went for the doorknob. She picked it up, figured she'd sweep the shattered glass after getting the keys. The door creaked open. She reached.

"Hola, mistress."

The lanyard and five long, brown fingers were looped around Ava's wrist. Stumbling back, she swung the broom. She landed two strikes before the door flew open. She scrambled toward the living room, hitting her head on the hallway corner. She looked back, saw that woman coming in after her. She swung again.

"Ay, ay, mistress, I dislike being hit with this."

"Get away!"

"Red, mistress. Rojo."

"Someone help! Help!"

"I am your dog…" the woman grabbed the broom. "…but this is too literal."

Ava staggered into the living room, patting her pockets for her cellphone. She whipped the silvery case up to her ear.

The woman's teeth were pointy and jagged when she grinned. "May other partners play with me later, mistress? We've only reunited."

"The hell you talkin' 'bout?"

She slipped a black duffel bag off her shoulder, tossed it toward Ava and set the broom on the floor. "I brought your favorites. The thick purple one would fit the harness you bought earlier."

Ava couldn't get a call to connect. She mashed buttons but the brick wouldn't light up.

"I apologize for keeping you waiting, mistress. You traveled much further from our last dimensional plane than expected. Not that mistress needs to explain, but I do wish to understand why you came here. It's an unremarkable, hard-to-find timeline."

Ava's phone dropped out of her hand.

*Mommy fetish over there is gonna chop my ass into pieces with whatever she brought in that bag.*

"Mistress?"

*Fucking Steve and that cat! I should've set all those damn flip flops on fire!*

"Mistress?"

"My name is Ava." She gritted her teeth. "Not mistress."

"Yes, I should've asked." The woman's black hair touched the floor when she bowed. "Mistress always chooses a new name to make each life cycle special."

"You just gone keep on with that, ain't you?"

Her head snapped up. "Oh. I see."

"See what?!"

"You've made yourself forget again." She shifted. "Do you enjoy growing into remembrance that much?" She plopped onto the couch.

Ava hedged toward the front door.

"You had to have felt me coming. After I picked up your scent, I sent five telegraph pulses through space-time. You must remember something. At the store it seemed like you knew I was yours to play with."

"Baby girl, I got no clue who you are."

She deflated, looking so pitiful Ava somehow felt guilty. "Hey, uh, I don't really get all this but, what if we picked up another time? Who knows? Maybe I'll remember something tomorrow. I'll take your number. What's your name?"

She groaned. "I don't have a name until you give me one. Even if it's the same one you always give me, it's not mine until you say so." Gray clouds manifested over the woman's head. They swelled with flashing electricity. "Mistress is always mistress, goddess of consciousness, duchess of time-space. I am her dog and I obey all her laws. Even if she doesn't remember writing them!"

The thunderclouds hailed.

"I will sit nameless on this couch until Ava defines me. Like I did in 1670, 2320, Lightyear Alpha, Lightyear Beta, and Big Bang Zero Hundred. Oh, the things mistress makes her dog endure."

The hail grew larger. Ava stepped back.

"This is not an agony which pleases!" She shook balled fists.

Ava sucked her teeth. "Elena. What about Elena?"

The iron-gray thunderclouds vanished.

"Imma take that as a yes?"

She shook ice from her long black hair. "'Tis the name Ava always gives her—"

"Stop callin' yourself my dog." Ava smiled politely. "Now then, since your name's all settled, let's get you out of my apartment, 'kay? Here we go." She gripped Elena's wrist, herded the girl forward.

She laughed. "Mistress is funny."

"No. Mistress is not funny."

"But you've made it so that Elena cannot leave."

Ava looked past the living room couch and froze. The kitchen, hallway, front door, all of it disintegrated.

Elena patted Ava's hand. "It's moments like these when growing into remembrance bothers mistress, too. You didn't realize you were changing things?"

Sweat beaded along Ava's temples. "You buggin'. This got your thundercloud demon ass all over it."

Elena narrowed her eyes. "Am I a demon now?"

"You would know."

"Mistress, you define *me*." Elena bit her lip when Ava

scowled. "I apologize. I've called you mistress for two hundred life cycles."

Ava pointed at the dark. "You didn't do that?"

Elena shook her head.

"You a damn lie. You were doin' magic earlier."

"Magía, mistress? I do not believe I am presently a witch."

"Those thunderclouds, hail and lightning, what you call that?"

She chuckled. "Mistress made it so that I could manifest my feelings visually. Eso no es magía. It took me time to learn how to speak after transmuting from canine form. You thought it would be easier to understand me this way."

Ava steadied herself with deep breaths. "I made the kitchen, the door, and the rest of the building disappear?"

"Sí."

"How?"

Elena stuck a hand into her duffel bag. "Through a shift in reality. That is what mistress controls as the goddess of consciousness." She pulled out jute ropes that, despite the confusion, made Ava's libido stand at attention. "Since I cannot leave, Ava will want to confine me for her own safety."

She set the ropes on the floor, turned around, and folded her arms behind her back.

Ava had slid into some dms, but this was beyond what she intended when she made her dating profile. "How you know I won't strangle you with these?"

"I like asphyxiation play." Elena looked over her shoulder. "But you've only done so at my request. Mistress may forget, change her name, live a whole new life, but mistress is always herself."

There it was again, that electric flower blooming within Ava. Elena's dark eyes were filled with a hunger Ava felt drawn to feed. Images flooded her mind.

Deep, lush kisses, glistening skin, hot tongue sliding down brown neck until teeth bit down hard.

"Does mistress wish to take me now?" Elena stepped close. "I'd be pleased to do what she envisions."

Ava staggered back. "You saw that?"

"I always see what you see when you tap into our memories."

Elena's arms were bound behind her back. Last Ava remembered, she was standing by the coffee table holding the ropes. "How'd you do that?"

"I didn't."

The way the jute framed Elena's breasts. Ava almost drooled.

"Gote shibari is your favorite box tie," Elena said. "Yes, mistress is always herself."

Ava sank into couch cushions.

"May I sit beside you?"

"Ain't like we goin' anywhere." Ava's bay window, coffee table, and couch remained, but the ceiling, bookshelves, pictures, plants, and lamps, all of it melted into vacuum. She couldn't see Oakland on the other side of the lake. The orange sunset turned lavender. Green, stagnant water evaporated into pixelated specks that whirled into a glittering cyclone.

All of this had to be that final hallucination the brain created when close to death. Tears beaded at the corners of Ava's eyes. "I don't want to die."

"Then you won't." Elena rested her head on Ava's shoulder. "This can simply be like that moment before you open your eyes after dreaming."

Ava lay her cheek upon Elena's soft hair. "What do we do now?"

She snuggled closer. "We open the door that takes us to

all the timelines. That's where we always start your journey into remembrance."

Elena's smooth skin was grounding. Ava's pulse quickened. She slid her fingers along Elena's cheek, tucked back long, black strands and rested her hand on the nape of Elena's neck. "Show me."

She closed her eyes. "Goddess of perpetuity and inimitable change, we call upon thy power."

Ava's toes grew hot. Heat traveled up her ankles, calves, thighs.

"Grace us with thine favor and grant us access beyond the veil…"

Fiery current rose into her belly.

"…so that we may know and serve thee throughout shifting form."

The scorcher shot up Ava's neck, into her face, pooled around her lips.

Elena straddled Ava's lap. Body pressed against body, Ava stared into dark eyes.

"Kiss me," Elena said.

She didn't hesitate.

They fell, Ava's arms wrapped around Elena, hands stroking the binding rope. Lips pressed, opening, wetness, fire, starlight and sun, scent of saffron and lime, resounding bells and whistling wind. Streaking, plummeting, embrace of water.

Sink.

Sink.

Sink.

Gasping for breath, Ava on top of Elena, Elena on top of red silk sheets. They rested on a four-poster bed full of plush red pillows. The blaze in Ava's lips blew out. Spools upon spools of oversized film unraveled through the air. The negatives were three times Ava's size. The ribbons of film were infinite. They spiraled and undulated through white space.

Besides the bed and the film, there was nothing else here.

"This is your projection booth. If it pleases mistress, think about your apartment."

When she brought her bay window to mind, one of the ribbons of film nosedived, whirled around the bed, spun until it flashed white. Suddenly the bed sat in the middle of her Oakland apartment living room. The shopping bag from Sultry Sensations was still on the coffee table.

She grabbed it and Elena's duffel bag, closed her eyes. The bed was back in the projection booth when Ava peeled her eyelids open.

Elena squirmed. "Mistress." She wrapped her legs around Ava's waist when Ava pulled the harness out of the tissue paper. "Please."

The fabric of Ava's t-shirt and jeans unstitched itself, billowed around her body and reformed into a red silk robe. A ribbon of film shot down and hovered beyond the mattress. A stereo eased out of one of its negatives. The film danced away, and Jodeci's *Forever My Lady* played softly.

"Please what, Elena?"

She rocked her hips, breath becoming heavy. Redness in Elena's cheeks mirrored redness on her chest. Ava imagined her sleeveless, black maxi dress melting into a lacy bra and panties. "Please reward me, mistress. I worked hard."

Ava placed her hands on either side of Elena's head and leaned forward. Her heavy curls created a curtain around their faces. "I thought you were gonna teach me about everything I control."

She slyly smiled. "Control me first."

Ava smirked. She grabbed the harness. "I did want to use this."

"Then if it pleases mistress, please, please do."

# Ongoing List Of Exceptional Orgasms #3: Center Of Attention In Basement Sex Club

Gia K. Trenchard

I need to be wanted by men. I mean that
in both the upper and lower case of the word.
Both literal and conceptual. Real and imagined.
It is an unfortunate flavor to crave this much.
I've often wished its depth would swallow.
But sadly. It doesn't. Not until right after I've almost drowned.
Extinguished. Suffocated in thick pulse and thrust.
In grease and grunt. In and out. Ideally
in rapid succession. Ideally in both depth
and girth. In name and blood.

I don't know any of their names, but the 3 of them
are looking down at me like a plate of ribs.
Like a meal they are down to share
but only if they are sure each will get his fill.

And I am here for all their filling.
I am here for my knees pushed as far apart
as I can make them go. I am here to be wet

clay thrown and hollowed out to perfect circle
by his steady hand. And his. And then his too.
I am here for more hands than I can keep track of.

I am here for the mosh pit I always dreamed of.
Dissonant collision of slow warm breath against
hot slap of flesh. I am so comfortable
on a painted concrete floor. In places of sung
leather harness and the chime of metal rings.
All I've ever wanted to be was the song
all the boys wanted to sing. Both the call
and the response. To be the stranger
whose hold holds other strangers
as we fall all to pieces.

I'm saying there are some praise songs so loud
I must sing into more than one microphone at once.
I'm saying sometimes my whole body wishes
it could be my mouth. As his breath races across
his gritted teeth. As I feel him swell close
the white hot flash. As his friends cheer him on
like it's their joy dripping off my lips.

I'm saying I want to be the show that they talk about
like I'm not right here. The spotlight they wait
patiently to take their turn in. I'm saying,
if you get me in the right room, I can beg
for anything without shame.

# Latin Freestyle

David Matthew-Barnes

I remember the rhythm at night:

Your hips wanting mine,
to grind our street-smart
lust into the crush of summer
heat. The beat of lives
never fulfilled. In the dark you say,
"Keep it on
the QT, down low. Slow, go slow.
Just like that, baby. Yeah." I say,
"When you hit it,
I'm yours *siempre, chulo*."

Our love is different during the day:

The tattooed thug boys
in the park with their sparks,
ankle holsters, packing. They pick
up on the bad girls with halter
tops, hair spray, razor tongues.
I get sliced with fear as you present
me to your neighborhood, your
surrogate *familia*. They suspect

the whole affair is a white
joke. I try to laugh off their eyes, claims

of their tongue and territory. I sip from
a stolen bottle of O.E., aware I'm out
of my element, zone. My intrusion
is forgotten when I share a common love

for the music bumpin' from your sound
system. It makes us dance at Southside, makes us
forget about zip codes, colors, rivals. Makes us pound
and throb like the concrete threat of imagined guns
to our heads, knives to our throats. We know that
when the song is over, we will bleed

for each other. Slowly.

# I Want to Watch Her Mouth the Word Umami

LeAnne Hunt

and think of butter dripping down my chin.
Of steam rising. A blush along my cheeks

as I think of teeth biting into bread pulled apart,
open and waiting. Remembering how I sank

my mouth into pot roast and understood
how muscular an action swallowing can be.

I've missed how a mouthful is nourishment,
of how lips purse to cool a mug of creamy coffee,

of how wrapping my palms around a cup is a prelude
to the sweetness, to the exquisite sensitivity of the tongue.

I am hungry to watch her mouth move thickly around
the word for savory. Mouth it for me again.

# Swallow It Whole

Sunni Jacocks (SJ)

Adam liked to choke me when he was close to the precipice. I liked that I could have been something to hold on to when he was falling.

When we kissed, I could taste many things: weed, coffee, desire, mostly; layers of it drenched all over his tongue. If I wasn't careful, I could taste old memories: Adam's first time learning how to ride a bicycle. The crushing weight of falling, failing, toppling over, scraping his knee. The care of that was quick; his father held him. Sometimes, my fingers would caress the long-faded pale scar when I sucked him off. This wound was nothing compared to what he would experience as an adult, a memory he would never tell me.

He had many beauty marks along his body, going up from his stomach to his neck and face, some smaller than others, some brown, others pink, in various sizes. My finger would run across his skin, connect them like constellations, immediately losing count. I would often do this after we had sex, his chest hair tickling my cheek, my ear pressed to his heart, listening to how our breathing might sync.

With other partners, I could hear their coherent thoughts, complete sentences that ran together, thoughts of what they wanted to do to me, things that they didn't even realize they were thinking, buried deep, but at the surface. But not with Adam. In the post-sex state, he was at his most quiet.

He was already a person who didn't say much, granting me only a few words. To the outside observer, they might only hear the sighs of relief as I played with the beads of sweat on his happy trail.

But I could hear him, hear him when he held onto my hips—his cock sliding in and out of me—thinking, *girl, girl*, even though we've had multiple conversations about my gender. And he corrected himself, in his head and out loud, using the pronouns I told him. "They/them," when the "he/him" was too difficult to comprehend because my body said "girl."

But the pronouns that came with girl, the ones that inconveniently slipped out of his mouth and crowded his mind, communicated, and confirmed that this was the way he saw me. It did not matter when he told me otherwise, tried to push out the "good girl" with "good slut" when the word left his mouth. I saw the repeated image of me that played in his head, my moans forming into delightful screams that made his dick harder.

When we first started playing with pain—a slap on my ass to start, pinching my skin hard enough that I could feel it throughout the day—he was amazed that the bruises he had left healed in seconds.

At first, he thought something was wrong, that he did something wrong. His fist landed, a soft thud, gradually finding rhythm as he continuously pounded my ass cheeks like dough. I rocked forward on my hands and knees, feeling myself open up, releasing tension where I felt pain, giggles escaping me, and where I began to find stinging, that was when my breath found me. During moments like this, I would not exhale, "red."

Not with Adam.

We had been seeing each other for almost a year now. There were no expectations because we were casual, and that meant that there was nothing to keep, nothing to hold. It also meant that we would both let weeks go by without talking, let text conversations drop, and pretend like the other was not ignored. That was something he started, and I did not complain. It was easier. But this also meant that I removed myself, my body. Some people call it subspace, but in therapy, we called it dissociation. They are not the same thing, but I often found myself balancing both, confusing the two. But it made me not give a fuck, that one time with Adam, locked in a carnal state, as I let him splatter his cum all over my chest. Our arrangement, unspoken, let my feelings of shame dissipate. And when I asked for a towel, not expecting him to help me clean it off, loving how the thickness melted thinner, I sighed with delight, even when he expressed fear of dripping on the bed.

Although we played well together, Adam could only stay in this state for small moments. And I savored them, especially after we were done and he held me, his warmth pressed against me. And at the times he couldn't, I held myself.

He was aware of this and knew when he *should* have provided some support, especially since we were both playing with something so delicate, but in a casual encounter, there was an unspoken acceptance of, "I can never count on you."

And so, when his hand found my ass again, hitting it harder than he usually did, and continued, waiting to hear the soft escalation of my moans before hitting in the same tender spot, I knew this would be a mark that would stay. Except it didn't.

I knew it wouldn't. I had left marks on myself before that never stayed. This would be no different. But these markings, I wanted.

"Uh, something's off," he had said.

"What do you mean?" I wanted him to say it.

"The color. It's disappearing."

"Hit it harder," I told him.

"Are you sure?" he asked, concern in this voice.

Without moving my position, I turned my head, and said slowly, "Hit. It. Harder."

And then there was a shift. Adam, the man he was normally; lonely, sad. Nothing he would ever admit, pushed me down, so my ass was higher, and my face was pressed on the bed.

He hit me again, but this time, I could hear it, a slap that rang in my ears and vibrated throughout my body. There was no build. There didn't need to be. The feeling from earlier was still there, but instead of pain, it was a soreness that made everything else intensify. Adam smacked me a few more times, keeping his hand on my skin after each until the last one where he thrust his two fingers inside me. My clit was already hard and throbbing, aching to be touched, and so I let out a rapturous wail that came deep from the back of my throat.

Suddenly I was able to float—because I could hear Adam—nothing coming from his mouth but groans, listening to that and also the controlled, constant humming of his thoughts: *that's good. So good* (the image of me, the way he saw me, slowly allowing myself to beg, my tongue out, panting, begging for him). *Warm, so warm* (thinking about how rosy my ass was). *I love the way I feel inside you...I wanna see you.*

And so, I turned around for him. He didn't ask and did not know I could hear him, but his thoughts said: *such a good slut. You know what I want.* And I did.

He grabbed my face with his other hand, squeezing my cheeks together, forcing me to look up at him. His eyes, once soft, found strength, found a longing to destroy what was in front of him. He wanted to wreck me. I knew he was getting harder; his mind focused on how that control felt.

He had me on my knees, waiting for another command that I knew was already coming. My eyes were still on his and I heard the familiar sound of the zipper of his jeans.

"You like me taking control, don't you? My little whore," Adam said as his thumb slowly caressed my bottom lip. It's an ask for confirmation, a little bit of fear, anxiety that made him believe he had gone too far. He hadn't, and I nodded, comforting his concern, his thumb demonstrating what he would do to my mouth. His jeans were all the way down now, his cock fully erect and inches from me. He grinned wickedly. "Suck," he said.

I closed my mouth on him and, at first, there was the taste of fear, cold, shivering, eased by warmth. A memory of a relationship that had turned sour, him losing control, finding the courage to leave; a hunger to find power and pleasure.

"Good, good," he said, his eyes holding mine. He shoved himself deeper, my mouth widening for him.

He wanted to push me more. But he was worried; he didn't know if he would consume me. But that was what I wanted. To leave that plane, only for a little bit, and find relief in that, in being nothing but the vessel for his outpouring. There have been many times that I had not asked for that, asked to be somebody's dumping ground, a place to unload their burdens. Here, it was my decision. Adam was not safety, not comfort, but a dream, permission to escape, fall, unattached from reality. I knew this relationship would not last. Something cannot exist if the other is not willing to give what the other takes.

And so, I ate up every hope unfilled, every dream faded and forgotten, every frustration from the job that felt like something was missing, every night spent alone, every unanswered message he ever sent, every relationship that did not work out, every disappointment, betrayal, heartache, every shattered self, and every piece of him that was buried, parts that he did not even know about, and I swallowed it whole, and it tasted sweet.

# Letter to an Old Flame: The Upstairs Lounge

Steve Ramirez

i.

We wanted our love illicit: two parts Scarlet, one part Rhett and a hint of a high school Heathcliff in hot pants. We Braille'ed our way into love across the fog-strewn shore of a dance floor, hands and hips murdering our inhibitions one song at a time.

*You can't tell my parents,* you said as I took you in my mouth. Not the best time to make me laugh.

ii.

My parents found out the same way Columbus discovered America: accidental, irreversible. They didn't find anything new. It's been here the entire time, folks.

No father should walk in on their son, spelunking their best friend's cave, but he should learn to knock. We were still puzzling together these jigsaw bodies. How they fit. How they crash together. How they fall in and out of love like everybody else.

iii.

It's bad enough the wounds were self-inflicted, but the silence...? The laughter...? Our own families carving those names

into our foreheads with their eyes. Did it make it easier? Add distance between the men they thought we would become and the disappointment they imagined we were?

Do we ever love a person for who they are, or just paint pictures of them with our minds and hope it's enough?

# Talent

Alex B. Toklas

I'm face-down on the bedroom floor
keeping company with dirty socks
with underpants, and lotto stubs
and cautionary tissues.
They float between the creeping dust
and creaking futon frame
while I'm slowly taken over
by the movement of my jaw
recalling entrances and exits
of uninvited cock.

I'm thinking about singing
on this narrow strip of ground
on a timeline without adjective
because Möbius was a proper name
with no relative perspective
only charismatic arguments
for opening my mouth a little wider.

"You have such enormous talent.
Let me show you all the ways that I
can help you with that break in your voice."

Two short pulses stop the spell
and I'm pulled back through my hipbone
ribs to shoulder, up on forearms
finding glasses, thumbing screen.

"You made me cum with your left hand."

I won't answer right away
I let my cheek drop through the floor –
through the molten recollections
of the night before.

I cup hand to joining legs
I leverage forearm against elbow.
I push hard against their places
fingers teasing lips to open
even though I make them leave their boxers on.

I feel them grinding on my palm,
harder pressure, never yielding
my thumb against their hard-on
slow vice, the way they like it
They're bucking hard, they're calling out
and I can't believe it's real.

"Fuck.
Fuck.
Fuck.
Fuck.
Fuuuuuuuuuuck…"

"Really?"
Do you like it?

Really?
Do you feel good?"

I give up my hand and
let my lips taste their brow,
their eyelid, perfect ear and chin,
their absent Adam's apple.
My nipples graze their chest
but I can't kiss them on the mouth
and when their hands move up my body
I try my best to form a hollow.

I know it isn't me,
it isn't me that they've been fucking,
but every single violation,
of that 13-year-old's voice.
Capturing his body,
as I hover overhead.

I can't tell them.
I can only kiss them
through evacuating pleasure
when they're holding on to nothing,
not even me.

# Timbales en el Cuarto de Tula

## Lisbeth Coiman

I.
As your cuerpazo leans forward over me
to say goodbye
I want to
massage my fingers
in the red sand of your head
Bathe in your hazelnut eyes
Explore the burnt sugar on your skin
without a compass

Heart beats fast
Lips brush earlobe
Tantalize the taste bud
with the desire to bite yours

Explosion of sensations
licking fingers of the hand you held

II.
Don't you ever talk in my ear again
with that baritone voice of yours
if you will not call
me tomorrow

III.
Last night in my sleep
I reached for the place
where your hand rested
as we said our good-byes

Sensitive to the touch
the spot burnt with the memory
of your fingers on my skin

Today I reach for the arnica
in the medicine cabinet
because I'm not calling you to
ask you to take care of this burning

IV.
I'm manifesting love with you
like conjuring a prayer
Kneeling in front of the only saint I worship

My lips imploring
to quench this thirst

V.
I wish you were          weed
to
inhale     you
Fill my lungs with the essence of you
Hallucinate          harmony
Giggle               as your drumming
fingers     discover tropical rhythms
my hips     dancing in duet
with your smooth voice

Timbales in El Cuarto de Tula of my eardrums
Lick the burnt sugar                         off your body
Munch on your finger            tips
Drink

# Prick

## Arwyn Carpenter

1. *Listen. Lie on your belly, hands to the sides. Press your hips down; find that alert twinge and stay still. Wait for me; don't move; keep pressing down.*

I like to see you naked from behind. You have no idea. I've told you about the living night seas of your white ass, but you can't know the humanity there. The personhood. The loveliness. Another face to gaze at.

*Still waiting, yes? I know you're getting wet because you know I want you ready for me. You're a good boy.*

*Listen. Can you hear me unbutton my shirt? Hold your breath until I say.* I slide my arms out of the sleeves. *Hear the tiny hairs catch the cotton?* The hairs on your legs prick and stand on end.

*Okay breathe,* and you do, but with shallow sips, not knowing what's to come. I start at your feet. I'm a glutton for your toes, sticking each one deep in my mouth. Not touching. Not biting, yet. Enveloping and closing my lips around each base, keeping back my tongue. All you feel is hot empty space.

I fold your legs, hold your feet in my hands and kneel up against your bent knees. *Let's stay here, face down, good boy.* The big toe of one foot, then the other, popping alternately between my lips, I kiss them dryly, keeping back the wet that will come.

You start to move your hips, but I haven't said okay. *Please* you beg into the mattress.

*You need to move your hips, angel? You need more pressure on your little cock? You can move, go ahead, that's it. Now stop, stay still my love, stay still, listen.*

I stand up on the bed, straddling your milky legs and you hear the pull of the leather strap, the harness buckle. You strain to see which cock I'm readying. *Eyes down my love.*

2. We are both new to this queering, this trans-ing, this kinking. There is so much we haven't yet imagined. This is the first time I'm giving commands and you are taking them and the rough assuredness of my voice shoots through my sex like a current. You've been almost patient, not quite though. I saw you twitch and meld your hips deeper but now you've been holding still for me like I asked. *My good monster.*

Standing on one foot, I run the other from your neck down the very center of your spine. I stop with toes hovering over your crack and grip in. You writhe and buckle. I grip harder, release, and slap you gently with all five toes spread wide. It's paining my dick not to slam down into you, to go this slow. Being so new, my young cock's eager, just learning to wait. I part your perfect ass with my toes.

3. *What if we stop here?* I ask, the smooth pad of my big toe held firm on the softening squint of your hole. Your ass perks back. You arch and hold. Your hole swallows the entirety of my toe.

4. *Fuuuuuuck* you moan and thrash once like a shark, your gripping sphincter is your teeth. Against the harness, my pussy pulses hard twice. My knees weaken, wobble, my toe slides gently deeper into your squeeze.

You stop moving and so do I. We hold, we hold. I see you relax. Breathe out… expand, expand then immolate and whimper as I slowly twist, rotate my foot, dragging against your clench, small toes across your cheek.

5. Seeing your peeking pale neck strain between the curtains of dark mane: you are a river of pleasure for the eyes. I long to put my lips there on the whiteness. The longing wrenches my cock. *Release me my good boy.* Obediently you turn molten; I slip out and kneel across you at your waist. You feel the tiny metal tongues where the harness scrapes. You still haven't seen which cock I've got on, though it slaps at your back when I lean down like a vampire, all teeth on flesh, to eat your neck.

You wiggle in my straddle. *My good boy likes this doesn't he?*

*Please, yes, please.* I swallow your ear, licking into the curves, and move to mouthing the bone of your jaw.

My hands are working behind your head, scratching at your scalp, fingers combing through strands, gathering your loose tail into one fist, and I try something new, a quick little tug. You gasp, our eyes lock. *Is this okay?*

*Yes, please, please.*

*Like this?* I tug again more sharply.

Your eyes go round, glassy, and you nod, surprised at the way you like it. A shiver runs over my shoulders, and I release. I lie down beside you. We are face to face. We speak into each other's mouths, but we haven't yet kissed.

*What if I fuck you from behind while I pull your hair?*

Again, you nod intensely into my eyes, begging for it. *Please do that, please fuck me, and pull my hair.*

*You want that, monster?*

*I need that please, please, please.* Each time you say the word I feel it in my mouth—the sibilant vibration on my tongue—our mouths open but not touching—breathing, holding.

*I could cum right now, you are so beautiful,* I growl into your open mouth.

*Please*, you pant, *cum for me*.

*No, let's wait, I want to wait with you. You can wait, right, angel monster?*

You look down and see my cock. It's the veiny pink one with the fat head that stretches you—the one we both love. You take it in your hands, moan and fall against my open mouth. We kiss softly with slow control, my fingers back in your hair. Mid-melting, I give it a tug and your gasp pulls the air from my throat.

We kiss hard now, and our hips move into each other. We take turns sucking each other's tongues, licking each other's teeth, pressing each other's lips open wider. More frantic, frenzied, hard, harder until we are mouth fucking. This fucking is the kind where we feel our love the closest—talking and fucking—pressing love into each other's mouths.

Oh, this bliss of kissing like this—breathing each other's breath. *You are so powerful,* you tell me.

*Do you like that?* I ask.

*Yes.* And again, the shiver of new discovery—my power, jangles straight down my spinal column.

6. *I'm ready, Daddy.* It shocks me to hear the word. You've never called me that before. Blood rushes to my ear.

*Am I the Daddy?* I ask.

*Would you like to be?*

*Yes,* I say, and the shiver drops lower to a pulse where my Daddy cock and balls would be.

*Do you want me like this?* You fix me with round eyes and move to all fours, then drop your chest to the bed.

*You look so beautiful my angel, my good boy, let me look at you.* I move behind you. This new way of looking at you has me transfixed. More than anything I want to sweep my cheek across your ass, to lay my ear against your hole, to listen to the inside of you.

7. *Are you going to fuck me, Daddy?* Again, it strikes me sideways

to hear my new name—a heady power. The sweetness in your voice gets me swirling, undulating, priming to thrust.

*Yes, my boy, Daddy's going to fuck you. Are you ready for me?*

You convulse, a wave through your spine ending with a jut of your hips up and back, such an alert, intelligent ass. *Please Daddy, I'm ready.*

I tongue into your pussy, gather your divine secretions, sweep them up over your anus and tongue them around.

*Ahh ha god yes, please.*

I focus in on your hole, how I've wanted to enter you here, to feel you pull me in. Slick and tight. I press in with my tongue, only the tiniest tip but you clasp and hold, you hold me there so we can feel this together. I am mesmerized by your pulling on my tongue, your grasping. Inside I can feel every ridge. I push slowly upwards. This muscle is tightly swollen. I push to the right, drawing the slowest circle, feeling each direction of this thrilling miracle.

*Please Daddy,* you whimper, *please I need you.* I breathe in through my nose, let my tongue thicken and plunge in deeper. You are a squirming pleasure dream.

8. Until now I've kept my hands to myself, doing the work with mouth alone but my fingers are cramping with need, so as lightly as I can, without changing the pressure of my tongue,
I run flat palms up the lengths of your thighs, and back down.

I can tell by your fitfulness that you're aching for the smack. Just thinking about how hard I will hit you, how instantly the redness will rise to show the exact mapping of the sting. Just thinking this starts a contraction in my belly—the receding before the tsunami.

You grind your face into the pillow as I begin to withdraw my tongue, my hands still hovering over your thighs. *I'm going to hit you now.* With my full power, I steady and aim at the roundest flank of your ass. Thwack.

The sound you make is a broken cry; it guts me to hear, but your words come out deadly clear.

*Again please, Daddy?*

*Good boy, my good monster, good boy.* I brush the hot red print with my lips. *Thwack, thwack, thwack.* You are stunned silent in the seconds that follow and finally gasp your inhale. It stuns me as well to take you to this place, to be this person to you, to watch you writhe and beg me for more pain. *I'm going to fuck your ass now.*

9. The harness has shifted and needs tightening. I like the pinch at my hip when I pull the strap wetly along my slit. I'm hard and the leather catches my tiny dick. When I dab the end of my fake cock with a spot of lube, my sex tightens as though to pump a bead of cum down the shaft. *Daddy wants to fuck you now.*

I've never seen you like this. You're taken over, possessed, writhing, spasming. *Shhh, my angel, hush now, Daddy needs you to lie still and answer me. That's a good monster. Good boy. Now, tell Daddy what you want.*

*I want your cock, Daddy, please.*

*You want Daddy's cock?*

*Yes, I need it, please, please.* You look back at me through your web of boy hair, pleading.

*You want Daddy's cock where?*

*In my ass! I want it in my ass!*

*Thwack*

*You didn't say please.* Your eyes round in shock as you realize your mistake.

*Thwack*

*Please, Daddy, please can I have your cock in my ass?*

*Right here?* And I smack a third time, keeping my hand where it lands and sliding the tip of my middle finger over your hole.

*Yes, please, Daddy, right there!* And I press in to feel you greedily swallow to my knuckle. I use my other hand to stroke my cock and spread the lube over the shaft. This action of gliding, jerking my prick with my hand, never fails to bring on a surge of hot transmasc joy. *My cock*, I think proudly, as I gave its pink length one last squeeze and bring its tip to your hole.

10. We haven't done this before. I've thought about it and thinking about it has made my cunt and anus convulse in tandem—hands-free.

*Daddy's going to push into you now. Ready?*

*I'm ready*, your voice has turned thick, *please, push your cock into me, push hard.*

I do exactly that. I push in, hard and deep, faster than I'd meant to—one serious thrust. I know it hurts you by how you go still and clench. You let out a moan that ends in a jagged cry. I hurt you. *I hurt you, my angel.* But your hands fly back from your face to land with sharp cracks on either side of your ass—you pull yourself open for me—you squeeze down—you swallow me in deeper.

Time stops. The universe is frozen cock, squeezing ass. Amazingly you begin to soften like oozing earth begging to be ploughed, to be dug into and filled.

And it happens: we're fucking. I'm fucking your ass—pulling back—thrusting hard—animal grunt after animal grunt. I'm fucking you with my tight tiger hips, my practiced buck. *I love this, Daddy,* you moan.

I fuck in and hold, I drop my weight into you. I fuck in again, hard enough to knock you on to your belly. Now I reach both hands up your back to gather your reins.

*Angel boy, my beautiful angel? Is it okay, the way Daddy's fucking you?*

Your *yes* comes up from your pussy, a guttural pained consent.

*Touch yourself my boy. Daddy knows you've been waiting. It's time.*

You bring the first three fingers of your right hand under and straight into your wetness—a thirst being quenched. You drag creamy salt juice over your red dick-clit. Your head jerks left, and you feel your hair tight in my fist. Oh, this silken grip, chunks of hair between each finger. I could yank hard, but I don't. I just hold you, as tight as I can, so you can't move.

I go back to my fucking. This is hard, fast. I'm thrusting from my glutes, from my prostate or where I imagine it might be—a tearing is coming up from my base. I feel as one with my prick, all my focus there—my dick, my proud pink stick—cramming you full again, again, again, again.

I release your hair and grab on—release and grab—release grab sharp twist. I can hear that you're about to cum in your voice—your cries take on shock, wet gasps. *Cum for Daddy, good boy, cum, cum for Daddy, cum my boy, cum...*

I realize the glass is rattling in the window frame with the intensity of your voice. Your deepest, hardest, most devastating cry. Your beautiful body is thrashing. Six convulsions, eight, crescendo, ten. The sounds you make have started my trembling—tension gathering, this incredible place: tender, a brief starry stillness before pieces fly apart, tumbling giddy wild pleasure, glorious ecstasy.

My voice is a rumble: *Daddy's cumming. Daddy's cumming inside you. Daddy's cumming inside your ass my boy, my beautiful angel monster boy.*

11. There's that heat like a fever that comes on after I climax since I started on T. Your body is hot, too. I'm still inside you, my breasts puddling on your back. I rest my head. It has

changed me, what we just did. It has affirmed my trans nature: I'm a faggot and it feels so wholly right.

*Did you feel that? Did you feel how right that felt?*

We are back to you and I—done with names for now, just me and you. You are purring.

I tell you with pliant kisses how much deeper in love with you I've fallen again.

# Exhibits

Shari Caplan

Exhibit at 13

I'm alone with velvet couches and a lacquered
woman.

Ten minutes into a movie, the men spread below nudity,
eating her humanity.

I replay the scene until I'm compelled to tongue
the projectile wooden nipples of the statue.

An unvarnished animal
in the club lights of a screen.

Exhibit at 10

the sprinklers gushing
Josefina's towel hung open

a patch of curls creates heat tremors
that open the body

passionfruit cups its juice
I spill over

## Exhibit at 21

When I need a dose of the feminine physique,
I put on my man-goggles and get wet. I want
the want they want me to. A girl versus girl
kind of guilt.

## Exhibit at 30

Whiskey-colored horses wild on her hills.

She draws her hunger in circles
on my back. My husband a pulse
beneath the fabric.

All the cars we drove over licking
their leather for her.

## Exhibit at 27

Suits are to lingerie as injustice to America.
When my husband comes home in shirtsleeves
from an interview, I pine after the suit jacket
and ask for a reverse strip-tease.

# After the Two-Hour Scene of Coworking & Showering

Sinclair Sexsmith

this desire to be with you
itches, it pulls
at the pink layers
of me, underneath.
something needing
tended to, something raw
needing soothed. so
it was such a relief
for you to call, type
away at your work
while I journaled, while
I made altars
out of the blank pages
in my notebook

relief isn't the right word

what's the word for when
you are parched, so thirsty,
and you discover a garden hose
left on, pouring, spurting

in that perfect arc that water
makes with itself. what's

the word for when you aren't
alone in love, but met,
building kingdoms from
the intimacy of watching
how I do my hair, how you play
with yours when you're
frustrated. so, of course
I had to bring you with me.
after such relief, who
could separate when they
could escalate? you know
how lovers say

has anyone ever been in love
the way we are in love? and
they haven't—ever—because
they have never been us, now
and this, this is the time
when it's happening. I am
relieved, in the way of students
receiving praise from the one
mentor they admire. in the way
of shelter dogs when they wake
and find their bowl filled. so come

watch
how I slide a blade
across my cheek
and chin, how my wet
hair is so much darker

how I look at myself
when no one is looking
except
you were, this time

you were

and it is a continued
joy, privilege, slice
to my underbelly,
the way you look at me
like your eyes are lit
from inside, like you're
studying the shapes
my arms make
when I gather myself
back up, scoop all the gold
from where it's been
scattered, and bathe again
in the return of all
I used to think was lost.

# Tonto's Love Notes

Byron Aspaas

You don't know          I take photos every morning—
each blink, a captured moment
preserved, the landscape left

barren with absence. Satin
ripples          below stolen breaths—

each movement          echoes
          silent birdsongs          echo.

Sunlight pricks skin          golden,
a nettle field

grows unshaven          around the cleft
and          into contours of the land

of the mouth. The mask          you wear
nowhere—          turquoise stay hidden

behind eyes          sheeted. Yellow curls
imprinted with night;          the cap

nestles          behind the door
you entered;          swallows swirl

softly around                    my world
painted desert,            the flowers, sleep.

I wait—

# Detonated Acquiescence

Candice Reynolds

The world never seems to stop humming. The thrum of electricity from power lines and the low growl of car engines. The constant chatter of people, occupying almost every space you enter. It never stops.

On a regular day, I can make sense of these stimuli. I can sort the ambient noise from the sounds that keep me safe and that inform me. When I get stressed, though, I can't split them up. They ratchet up my stress levels; sound patterns grate at my skin and make me itch at invisible fleas. I flinch at sudden loud noises. I become a tight ball of muscle, hunched in on herself, reflexively shrinking inward to block everything out. Retaining control of my emotions, and appearing like a healthy and fully functioning member of society until I can get home, becomes my sole focus.

One such day, I staggered into my home. I kicked off my shoes and inhaled sharply, drawing in the scent of Arizona desert dust and remnants of the sandalwood incense my wife loves to burn.

The journey from the door to our bedroom seemed too far. So, instead, I let myself collapse onto the small couch in our living room. I pressed my face into the cool cotton weave of the sofa's arm and squeezed my eyes shut, doing my best to block it all out. I needed a release.

I woke with a start, as the cushion underneath me shifted and a hand brushed my bangs from my face.

"You awake?" My wife asked, perched on the edge of the couch.

I blinked my eyes into focus. I must have slept for at least a few hours, for her to be home from work now. Her lunch bag was on the floor and her work boots were still on.

"Mmmm." I groaned, blinking up at her.

"Are you feeling OK?" She asked. "This isn't normal for you."

I shifted my weight to help myself sit up.

"Bad day," I answered. "Anxiety got the better of me." I rubbed the back of my hand over my eyes to wipe the sleep away.

"Oh no, baby. I'm sorry." She frowned at me and rubbed my back.

I leaned onto her shoulder.

"I hate days like this," I whined, putting my hand on her leg. "I can't think clearly."

"We're going to have to do something about that, aren't we?" She spoke. I felt her pinch at the strap of my bra and snap it against my back.

It wasn't so much a question as it was a statement.

The sensation of her snapping my bra strap sent a chill over me. I felt the goosebumps creep from the top of my shoulders and down my arms and chest, peaking my nipples, turning them into hard nubs.

The corner of my mouth twitched.

"Yes," I answered, in a breathy exhale.

"Alright, then." My wife stood. "I want you to get into our bedroom. Everything off except for bra and panties. NOW." She punctuated that last word with a yell, making me flinch.

My limbs felt clumsy, but I stood as quickly as I could, head down, and rushed into the bedroom.

I heard her rustling in the kitchen, putting away the bits from her lunch kit. Normally that was my job.

"You better be out of that dress by the time I get in there, babe." I heard her call out to me. The dull thud of her boots being dropped on the shoe tray by the door startled me. Taking her boots off when she got home at the end of the day was normally my job, too. My fingers shook and I struggled to maintain my grip on the zipper head and to pull the zipper down the side-seam of my dress.

"Oh, baby. I'm disappointed." She spoke from our bedroom doorway, shaking her head.

I had gotten out of my pantyhose—they were balled up at my feet. The violet cardigan I had worn as a light jacket was crumpled beside it. My periwinkle sheath dress, however, was hanging from my hips. I had wriggled my arms out but had not managed to push the skirt down and step out of the garment.

I stood still as my wife approached me. She reached out and took hold of the waist of my dress and pulled it down to the floor. I met my wife's gaze. Her green eyes, the color of dried thyme leaves, searched my greasy Atlantic Ocean blue eyes.

"On the bed. Face down, for daddy." She commanded, her voice firm.

I stepped out of the dress and climbed onto our bed, crawling up far enough so that I could lay flat, but would not be propped up with pillows.

Almost as quickly as I lay on the bed, I felt a sting across the back of my thighs; the strike happened so quickly I didn't even register the sound of the riding crop whipping my skin. Nor did I have time to register that a second strike was likely to fall, before I felt the sting radiating from my skin.

"One for not meeting me at the door," She spoke clearly. "And one for not being ready for your chores."

I heard her tap the crop against her palm.

"I think you deserve another." She tapped the crop on the bottom of my foot and my leg kicked involuntarily. She knew I was ticklish.

"You didn't get undressed in time, baby." She grazed the crop up my heel, over the ridge of my Achilles tendon, and stopped.

"What do you think, love? Do you deserve another?"

"Yes," I responded.

"Louder."

"Yes, daddy," I answered with a clear voice.

Without any hesitation, I felt my wife strike the spade-tip of the riding crop on the flesh of my upper right thigh. My leg jerked. The strike was meant to hurt, and it had.

I heard my wife drop the riding crop into the antique trunk at the foot of our bed. The hinges of the trunk lid creaked as she closed it.

"Your discipline is over with, babe." She announced, coming around the side of the bed. I felt her fingers trace the outline of the spade mark on my thigh. The goosebumps that had come over me earlier washed over my body again.

"Now, it's time to get you out of your head." She pressed a kiss onto the hot skin.

"Thank you, daddy." I reached out to grab her hand and tugged lightly. She bent down, understanding the intent behind the gesture.

"Yes, baby?" She smiled.

I let go of her hand and slid it onto the back of her neck instead, pulling her towards me so I could kiss her.

"I need to let it go." I whispered to her.

"I can help with that." She broke the kiss, smiled at me,

and then, to my delight, she smacked my ass. I giggled and rolled over onto my back.
I watched as she took off her clothes, first her jeans and then her t-shirt and sports bra. She kept her boxers on, before going back to the trunk.

I scooted up the bed and laid back on the pillows while I waited for her.

When she finally got onto the bed, she was sporting black strap-on boxer shorts and an unconventionally colored dildo.

"As much as I love these," she slid a finger under the lacy elastic of my panties, sliding her finger over the crease of my thigh and my pelvis, until it grazed the soft fluff of my pubic hair. "They need to come off." She hooked her finger, the gusset of my panties trapped in the catch, and pulled them down between my thighs. I wiggled to help her get them off me the rest of the way.

"Sit up, take that bra off, and put your legs together." She commanded.

I did as I was told. As I unhooked the clasp of my bra, I watched as my wife took the panties I had just been wearing and wrapped them around my ankles, tying them in a knot.

I threw the bra I had been wearing onto the floor, and my wife slid her hand into the gap between my ankles. She skimmed her hand up between my calves, running it up along my knees, gliding over the soft skin of my thighs, before cupping my core in her palm.

The sensation of her warm hand meeting my center made my belly tense and pull taught. I laid back down, just in time to feel her press her palm down onto my clit. She put her weight behind it, grinding it down hard as she straddled me. Her wrist motions were short and controlled. She knew my body well.

"Fuck, yes," I moaned, leaning my head back into the pillows, but reaching my arms up to grab her thighs.

"Oh!" I startled as she pushed harder, while hooking her pointer and middle fingers down and pressing them inside of me.

"So wet already." My wife marveled, her fingers sliding in and out of me easily. "I bet this won't take long," She hissed, licking the skin between my breasts.

The sensations I felt on my body struggled to grab hold of me. My back arched and I moaned. I could feel the slick of my own wetness on my thighs, the restriction created by the panties binding my ankles, the throb of my clit growing harder under the pressure of my wife's palm, and the exquisite gentle thrust of her fingers.

"Almost there, hmm?" She kissed a scar above my right breast. She flicked her tongue up, and I felt the edges of her teeth on my skin. She bit down on my collar bone.

A mewl escaped my lips as I felt the pressure of her teeth, and then, suddenly, pressure on my hips.

"Sweet Je—" I sputtered, but my words got caught in my throat as my arms were suddenly pinned above my head.

"Fuck!" I yelped. My wife's hips thrust forward, and I felt the dildo she was wearing become fully sheathed inside of me. My thighs were already squeezed tightly on account of my ankles being bound, but my wife's glorious thighs squeezed them together even tighter. She ground her hips into mine, just as she had ground her palm into me only moments earlier. Her thrusts were deep, her hips moving in fluid motions that made me all but melt into her.

"Look at me." She continued to thrust, tightening her grip on my wrists.

"Please, daddy," I whined, unable to comply.

"Look. At. Me," she growled.

My body swam in confusion. Sound competing with intense physical sensation. I felt sweat and tears running down the side of my face. I was overwhelmed.

"Please Daddy, make it stop," I cried "Please."

"I can make it stop." She spoke sweetly, the growl gone from her voice. She kissed my chin. "Just look at me." Her hips pressed and rocked, the motion quickening.

I blinked away tears and struggled to see clearly, but my eyes locked on my wife.

"Good girl." She smiled at me. "Such a good girl." She kissed me and nipped my lip.

"Now, daddy?" I whispered.

"Now, baby. Let go."

My eyes were open, but all I could see was blinding white light. The white light seemed to burn me from the inside out. The heat traveled from deep within, unfurling like flower petals extending to greet the sun. There was no sound. I could not register physical sensations. There was no scent of sandalwood and desert, and no taste on my tongue.

Everything stopped.

And I smiled.

# Lemon Drop (song lyrics)

Natalia J

My buttercup got me, meltin' in the sun she
Shining all over the place
Her eyes piercing, bold and fiercely
Kissin' all over my face

I love it when you smile wide, cutie-cutie clementine
Ticklin' all on my insides
Wild n' sweet thang, baby girl booty tang
You the sky that's takin' me high

My Lemon Drop, my tangy lady, my Lemon Drop stops my heart
My Valentine, she mighty fine, I don't even know where to start
Lolli lolli, Lady Pop, lickin' gettin,' all the spots
Take my hand, to candyland, why you ask?
Because we can

Tangled in my mangoes, curlin' all my ten toes
Tropical your areas baby
Hot and bothered once again, butterflies of mighty kin
Flutter in my tummy lately

Electric type of rides, driving currents up my spine
Divine

Runnin' laps in my mind, sprintin' to the finish line
Winnin' in our own time

In between those thighs, oo oo she cries
Grippin' me all sorts of tight
Hourglass healthy, curves so wealthy
Rich is her flavor inside

My Lemon Drop, my tangy lady, my Lemon Drop stops my heart
My Valentine, she mighty fine, I don't even know where to start
Lolli lolli, Lady Pop, lickin' gettin,' all the spots
Take my hand, to candyland, why you ask?
Because we can

Twinkle twinkle, titty sprinkles
Batterin' all of your cakes
Gettin' really silly, on your filling
Ladi ladi lady-dazed

Snow White disarming, Princess Charming
I'll come awaken you sleepyhead
Fantasy Fairy Tale, panty-free on the real
Breaking spells royally on the bed

My frisky metaphors, are to the ladies I adore
Abundance of cheesiness, melting
Into a puddle, on the double
Your loveliness is overwhelming

My Lemon Drop, my tangy lady, my Lemon Drop stops my heart
My Valentine, she mighty fine, I don't even know where to start

Lolli lolli, Lady Pop, lickin' gettin,' all the spots
Take my hand, to candyland, why you ask?
Because we can

# Serengeti at Midnight

James Coats

You move as moonlight,
flickering blinks through glazed eyes.
Red pearl rising,
growing larger in heaven,
pulling me into you,
to work your cool defiant night on me.

Heat radiates from my core, natural attraction roars.
Let me spoon that smile into me like cereal before sunrise.
Let me drink the pleasure of your bubbling laughter
while you plant safety in my belly, and I grow trusting.
Vulnerability from the ends of my fingertips,
there is power in the indulgence of release.
Honest intentions spring up,
acacias sprout from golden tongues.
Soft petals lift and fold as leaves in the wind,
carried across the savanna us two lions.
All muscle, bare skin, and fierce hunger
surrendering to an audience of cheering stars.

Eyes hunt for tender passion,
lips pursue an opening to inhabit,
finds anticipation lingering on flesh

resting between crease of shoulder and neck.
Kisses migrate across this longing landscape.

Your hand explores your own desire
before replacing your digits with mine
showing me the right speed
of pulsing revolutions,
midnight's blue breath rising higher, higher,
high enough to touch the canopy of clouds
as we lay on soft sheets of grasslands
'Til lightning strikes the right spot.
Spark to inferno in seconds,
thunderous moans crash a godly pitch,
and it sounds like my name.

Let me live in your rainfall,
in your dripping need,
in your warming wetness
before you monsoon my atmosphere,
flood it like the Zambezi river,
reshape contours of my face,
turn mouth into torrent,
chin into waterfall.

I want to stay here with you
until we become soil once again.
Let me live in your raining satisfaction.
Let me pool in your plains of pleasure,
and we will watch our pride flourish,
grow boundless and ancient for all time.

# An Innocent Brush of Skin

Aiden Rondón

He only meant it as a reassuring kiss.

Whatever had happened, it had been the weirdest argument he'd ever been involved in. Haerel wasn't sure how the situation had escalated that much and that fast. He recalled sitting down with Kaine, his roommate, and complaining of the fact that he could not take care of both of them all the time. He remembered calling him a work-addicted idiot. He recalled Kaine's expression hardening, his dark brows knitting together just barely, the cold sweat that came down his back, and some harsh words from Kaine's husky voice. He recalled saying that his intention was not to attack him, but that he was worried and wanted him to be well and healthy, but he could not keep looking after him all the time. He recalled tears and a blurred vision. A heavy sigh, a warm hand cleaning his face, and a sudden rush of courage deep down his chest. He recalled faintly tugging the other man's arm and bringing him closer.

After that, he wasn't too sure what had happened.

All Haerel knew was that he was laying on their shitty couch with Kaine on top of him, kissing him like a hungry wolf finally catching up to his prey after months without having a bite to eat. The pair of calloused hands running under his linen shirt made that more intense, their grip firmer on his sides the closer they got to his chest. Kaine seemed a bit too unaccustomed to the contact, but his tongue was eager to taste Haerel to his last drop. He moaned against the older man's lips and dragged him closer, hooked a leg on Kaine's hips to bring their groins closer, and took the chance to take a handful of his long brown hair as well. His locks were clean but just as rough as they looked. A pair of thumbs caressed his nipples gently, maybe too gently for what he expected from Kaine, and Haerel had to break the kiss with a soft giggle.

"That tickles," he whispered against Kaine's lips, "I'm not so sensitive there."

Kaine sent him a slightly puzzled look. He wasn't surprised, given how straight the man seemed until barely a minute ago. Haerel smirked, showing off his sharp fangs. "Keep going; you'll know it when I like something. I'm loud."

Seeing the stoic bounty hunter go from confused to bright red was the second that made the whole experience worthy. Maybe intent on discovering what that meant exactly, or because he was that touch-starved, Kaine claimed his lips again, and this time his hands wandered down his body, eager to touch every inch of skin within their reach. They anchored finally under his shirt, just above the waistband of his pants, and a pair of rough thumbs traced the edge of his hip bones oh-so gently … Almost out of sheer instinct, his hips rolled slightly, and his hand gripped Kaine's locks harder…

Kaine broke from the kiss with a groan, his eyes set on Haerel's trapped erection that poked shamelessly against his rock-hard abs. Those hands held him tighter than they had ever gripped a sword, almost as if he tried to keep him still. As if the slight brush of half-elf asscheeks against his cock was too much to handle. Kaine's blown-out pupils were the only push Haerel needed to unleash his chaotic nature once and for all.

"Hey, I have an idea. I think you'll like it." He sat up, almost straddling Kaine's hips, and brought a hand down to his breeches to undo the ties slowly, in case the other refused his advance. Kaine just nodded, sweat damping the point of contact between his hands and Haerel's hips.

"Have you ever rubbed dicks with someone else?" Haerel asked with the sweetest voice he could muster, given the boner bothering between his own legs and the fact that he was about to fish his roommate's out of his pants.

Kaine kept his mouth shut for a second. He licked his swollen and wet lips before he finally spoke. "Never."

"Would you like to try?"

Another second. Then a push to change their positions back to the original—Haerel on his back, with a cloud of black hair around his pale face, holding Kaine by the dick while his athletic figure trapped Haerel against their shitty couch.

"Yes."

"Get my clothes off, then."

Kaine got to it immediately. His hands were bolder by the second, getting rid of his shirt swiftly and bringing his pants all the way down and tossing them somewhere else in the tiny room. Haerel expected him to touch him or kiss him immediately once again, but instead, Kaine knelt up to take his own shirt off. Haerel felt the heat accumulating both on his face and rushing down to his erection with the motion, his eyes following greedily the hem of the dark clothing as more muscle and pale skin reached his sight. A long scar came to view, but Kaine didn't give him time to process anything else after he discarded his shirt and knelt between Haerel's legs, closing the distance between their erections.

"Shit," Haerel moaned as he wrapped his hand around both their shafts and started stroking. His hips thrust against Kaine's on sheer instinct, his free hand anchoring to Kaine's shoulder. Kaine hid his face on Haerel's neck, failing miserably to suppress a pleased sigh behind a pointed, sensitive ear.

The faint smell of soap mixed with that strange musk of Kaine, his comforting weight over his chest, the steady rhythm of his thrusts oh-so akin to the kind of fuck he craved so badly … maybe this was a mistake; maybe he should have asked for more. He craved so much more now.

"Haerel, fuck," Kaine grunted, breathing erratically against the sensitive skin. His hands slipped under his thighs and clung for dear life to the flesh.

But all he could do was grind harder against Kaine. Flick his thumb more around his tip. Bring Kaine closer with his legs, even if that meant he could not keep his grip over Haerel's thighs. Even if Kaine had to move his arms around to take a good grasp of his asscheeks and thrust his hips erratically against him, groaning to his ear as his seed spilled over Haerel's body. Just a few strokes more and Haerel followed him, making even more of a mess of his dirtied chest.

They breathed in unison for seconds that almost seemed eternal, Haerel with a stupid smirk on his pretty face, and Kaine, slightly blushed, with his eyes set on the semen flowing down the curves on the other's chest. He got even more flustered after Haerel placed a peck on his parted, cracked lips.

"Get off, I need to clean that up." Haerel stopped himself midway through raising his chest, and after a pause, added, "Unless you want an early dinner off of me."

# Charlie Brown Shares An Awkward Night With Linus

Ben Trigg

It begins with a late night return to their dorm room.
Linus, emboldened by unlocked desire,
makes the first move.
Feigning a loss of balance, he stumbles,
presses his hand against Charlie Brown's chest to steady himself.
He leaves his hand in place a moment too long,
looks into his friend's eyes, and smiles.
Charlie Brown laughs uncertainly at the possibility of the moment.
He initially pulls back as Linus's lips find his own,
but leans into the feeling of being wanted.
A lifetime of rejection from the little red-haired girl has left him ready for this.
He closes his eyes, imagines her lips, her hand on his chest.
Linus presses hungrily at epiphany, realizing the wrong sibling has been pursuing him all this time.
He thanks the Great Pumpkin for where this night has taken him
as red and yellow shirts fall to the floor.
Soon they are clothed in nothing
but nervous excitement and a small blue blanket.

# The Wife and Her Pastor

Amanda E. K.

Pastor Rick and his wife Anita stand at the front of the conference room, smiling behind their microphones like Donny and Marie. They're the self-appointed leaders of the annual Biblical Marriage Conference, and they're just wrapping up their opening address in front of more than 100 Christian married couples.

Miranda and Bryan—partners in a polyamorous arrangement—are the only people there who aren't married, though they're pretending to be. Neither of them is Christian, though they both grew up in the Church. For them, this conference is fantasy fulfillment for their religious-themed kink play. Bryan is playing the role of submissive pastor, and Miranda the pastor's dominant wife. (*For those of you who grew up in the Church, you can understand the appeal.*))

Pastor Rick flexes an age-spotted, yet fit-looking arm, illustrating what it means to build better marriages *Jesus-Style.* "At this conference," he says, "we'll help you identify the root cause of your marital issues. Once the root is exposed, you'll start to grow in ways you didn't think possible."

"We'll help the men become strong leaders, and we'll help the women embrace the importance of supporting their husbands as leaders," adds Anita, her blonde bouffant hairdo bobbing with every syllable.

Miranda shifts in her seat so that her knee-length skirt

inches up her legs, drawing Bryan's attention to the lace of her white thigh-high stockings. She writes something on the biblical marriage worksheet in front of her and slides it under Bryan's eyes. It reads: *Do you promise to expose the root and help it grow?*

Bryan traces his tongue along his parted lips as he reads Miranda's message. He writes beneath it: *I do.*

"Good boy," whispers Miranda.

A 50-something man at their table looks at them as though he knows exactly what they're up to. Miranda imagines that he keeps pornographic photos tucked in the pages of his Bible and that he's at the conference to try and put an end to his addiction.

Later that afternoon, Bryan and Miranda attend a breakout session called "Reigniting the Marital Fire." A small projector screen at the head of the room glows with the Bible verse from *Ephesians* 5:22-24: "Wives, submit to your husbands as to the Lord. For the husband is the head of the wife as Christ is the head of the church, his body, of which he is the Saviour. Now as the church submits to Christ, so also wives should submit to their husbands in everything."

"Now, some people look down on submission as if it were something demeaning, degrading or humiliating," says Pastor Rick with a glued-on smile. "But in a biblical sense, that isn't what submission in marriage is about at all."

"What a shame," Miranda says under her breath.

"Rather, a wife who submits to her husband is choosing to empower him to have the self-respect he needs," says Anita, beaming at her husband. She then asks the group to share examples of healthy submission from their own marriages.

A man in the back wearing a bowtie and suspenders says that he balances his wife's submissiveness by asking for her permission for independent social outings, like playing poker with the guys.

Bryan nods in agreement and says, "I get great feedback when I ask for my wife's permission, too. Her support of my wishes to wear her makeup and stockings feels very empowering." There's a palpable silence in the room. Pastor Rick and Anita stand frozen, smiles still glued to their faces as though someone pressed a pause button on them before they registered what they just heard. After a minute, Pastor Rick un-glitches to suggest that that may not be what they were getting at. "Does anyone else have an example?" he asks with a shaky laugh.

Miranda raises her hand. "My husband and I feel most connected when I submit to letting him pleasure me." As she says this, she fondles a whip-like tassel necklace hanging between her breasts.

Again, a confused silence from the audience. Several people ogle Bryan and Miranda with concerned stares. The couple next to them appears to be praying silently, their fingers linked in their laps.

Pastor Rick and Anita laugh nervously and call for a five-minute break.

Miranda leans into Bryan and says in a husky Old Hollywood voice, "You were such a good boy for speaking up, Pastor. You have so much helpful knowledge to share about submission."

"I live to please you," says Bryan, hungrily eyeing Miranda's tassel necklace that she's casually brushing along the palms of her hands.

"Although … I'm a little worried," says Miranda, "that I may be spoiling you by sparing the rod." She slaps the tassel with a steady rhythm against her breasts.

Unable to contain himself, Bryan sneaks his hand onto Miranda's stockinged knee, which she immediately slaps away with the necklace. "You know you're not supposed to touch unless I say so, Pastor," she whispers to him in a terse librarian voice.

Bryan looks at the floor like a scolded puppy. "Thank you for reminding me," he says. "I guess I forgot. All this talk about submission got me excited. I deserve your punishment."

"Let's just hope you don't forget again," says Miranda. "Or I won't be quite so nice next time."

"Yes, ma'am," Bryan replies with a half-moan. "I live to obey your commands."

Pastor Rick calls for everyone to return their focus to the topic of marital bliss. "Now folks," he says, his eyebrows jumping playfully up his face, "we all know marriage is hard work. Anita and I have been married for 30 years, and we've run the gamut of difficulties. You name it, we've dealt with it. I won't get into the gritty details, but believe you me when I say we haven't always been this cheerful, loving couple you see standing before you today. If you want to know how we overcame addiction, neglect, disrespect, affairs, and daily arguments, the answer is *God*. When you let God move in you and expand your awareness of his love and grace, and when you learn to swallow your pride and ask God to be used as his holy vessel, he will *fill you* with a servant's heart so that you won't be spit from his mouth, as he warns in *Revelation*. As the kids say, God is down to forgive your sins. He asks that you come as one with your spouse to the feet of Jesus to be used as tools in his holy hands. Dear brothers and sisters, when you come as one, you can be sure that God will reward you."

As Pastor Rick elaborates, Miranda subtly teases Bryan. When the pastor says to let God move in you, she rocks her hips slowly, almost imperceptibly back and forth in her seat. When the pastor says to swallow your pride, she molds her fingers around her throat, gripping it for just a second, then swallows audibly. When the pastor says to come as one, she squeezes Bryan's trembling thigh, stroking it so gradually that no one else could possibly notice her intentions. All this teasing has Bryan clutching his Bible and biblical marriage worksheets to cover up the holy expansion rising from the front of his pants.

"This is more erotic than the burlesque show we saw in Vegas," he whispers to Miranda.

"Shhh," she whispers back, touching her index finger to her lips.

"Now let us close in prayer," says Pastor Rick.

With everyone's heads bowed and eyes closed, Miranda slips her right hand between her upper thighs, just for a moment, then brings her fingers to Bryan's face, as though brushing a crumb off his upper lip. Bryan, seemingly moved by the spirit, blurts out, "Holy Jesus!"

Several people in the room, including Anita, echo him with convicted moans of "Yes, Lord!" and "Praise God!" Miranda covers her face so that no one can see her laughing.

After the session, as Miranda and Bryan are following the crowd to the main hall to debrief over decaf coffee and sheet cake, Miranda suddenly grabs Bryan's hand and pulls him into a hallway closet. This closet—which happens to be a pageant costume closet—is filled with togas, rope belts, angel wings, halos, and even a crown of thorns.

Miranda straps Bryan into a pair of lacy white wings and rests the crown of thorns atop her head. "Bow down and receive absolution for your sin of yielding to temptation," she commands, pushing Bryan to the floor by his shoulders.

"Yes, Madam Savior," utters Bryan, the bulge in his pants pulsing with fiery devotion. "Nothing pleases me more than serving you."

Miranda pats him on the head then wiggles her panties down to her ankles and tells Bryan to take and eat of her flesh.

"This is my body, given up for you."

After an entire day of delicious, agonizing teasing, Bryan is more than willing to partake in his lover's communion. He takes Miranda fiercely by the hips, burying his face in the fragrant folds hidden beneath the hem of her schoolgirl skirt where he bathes his lips in her anointing oil. "Please," he begs, "may I touch myself while I pleasure you?"

Miranda thinks about it while she pets his hair in rhythm with the caresses of his zealous tongue. "Yes, you've more than earned it," she eventually decides.

Within minutes, Miranda's back is arching, her hips bucking up from the box of prayer candles beneath her. Unable to keep quiet, she pulls out a rope belt from a tangled pile and bites onto it to stifle her orgasmic scream, removing it only to command Bryan to cum as she finishes. At her command, Bryan explodes onto a stack of glittering halos.

They take a few minutes to catch their breaths, smiling devilishly as they clean up the closet (after all, they're no philistines), then they smooth out their clothes and leave the closet one at a time to join the rest of the couples in the main hall.

Hand-in-hand, they walk up to Pastor Rick and Anita at the refreshment table. Bryan reaches out to shake Pastor Rick's hand and says to him, "My wife and I want to thank you for the positive impact you've had on our marriage in such a short time."

"It's true," adds Miranda. "Thank you so much for helping to ignite our fire. May God reward both of you for your service." Pastor Rick and Anita flash coy eyes at one another. "As a matter of fact, we'd like to thank *you*," says Pastor Rick with a wink in his voice as Anita passes a business card to Miranda.

"Please give us a call this weekend. Day or night. We'd love to express our gratitude for what you've brought to *our* marriage."

And with that, the pastor and his wife walk off to mingle with another couple, leaving Miranda and Bryan's imaginations whirring with new and unexpectedly thrilling role-play scenarios that they already can't wait to enact.

# Hide & Seek

Geneviève

*Oh, FUCK!!!*

Of all the hot hopes I'd had for this scene, losing the metal plug inside my boy's ass was definitely *not* on the list. Yet here we were, his ass skyward in our bed, and my eyes staring with disbelief at my nitrile-and-lube-covered fingers ... fingers which no longer had a hard silver flange, or *anything*, between them. I pinched them twice just to be sure I wasn't imagining it and felt my boy shudder as they nuzzled the sensitive and slick skin of his greedy ass. The affirmative reaction slapped my brain with cognitive dissonance as I felt my panic rising.

*FUUUUUCK. What do I do? How do I get the plug out? How far is it? Please don't fucking let us wind up on* "Sex Sent Me to the ER." *I am the Worst. Daddy. Ever. Wait, no. No, no, no. Be here now. He doesn't even know what happened yet. You have to get it out. The plug must not win.*

*Deep breath. Exhale. Okay. It can't have gone too far. He hasn't moved, his back is level. Do I tell him now? No, he's too far down into subspace. I don't want to panic him. I can do this. I can do this.*

I put my ungloved hand on his hip, gently stroking his skin. I hear him whimper. "That's my good boy," I murmur, trying to keep my voice purring the way it was before the plug rudely decided to go on a solo spelunk. "Now, Daddy needs you to listen to me, my good boy. Are you listening?"

"Yes, Daddy."

"Good boy. Now, I want you to bear down on my fingers, okay?" I gently press my sticky fingers against his asshole and feel him push back on me. I slip inside him; he moans and his breath quickens. I keep my hand moving on his hip in reassuring circles and concentrate on breathing steadily as I finally feel the solid metal flange.

*Oh, thank fuck.*

Slowly, I work to widen my fingers, both to stretch his ass again and to open them wide enough to grab the damn plug.

"Good slut, you like when Daddy stretches out your ass?"

"Yes, Daddy. Yes, oh *fuck*, yes." His breathing was heavy, trying to form words and not get lost in the sensation. Which was good. I needed him to be as present as possible. Once I am sure I have three fingers on the piece of metal I hate most in the world right now, I tell him to take a deep breath. He does so.

"Now, let it out." As he does, I slide the plug backwards, slowly, consistently, until I can at least see the silver of the actual flange again. I try not to collapse in relief, because it's *still* not all the way out.

"Another deep breath, my boy. Let it go." The widest part of the plug was all that had to come out. I focused hard on pulling it steadily, not yanking it out and flinging it across the room like I wanted to do. Finally, after what felt like weeks, the little silver fucker glided out, almost cute in the way it popped the rest of the way after the largest part was out. Rude.

I placed it down on the chux and took a deep breath to steady myself. I'd kept the tears at bay the whole time because it was an emergency Situation, capital letter and all. Now that he was out of immediate danger, I could feel the Daddy swagger evaporating.

"Good job, my sweet boy. How are you doing?" I asked. I *think* I handled it well, and quickly, but I wanted to make sure to check in with him.

"My ass feels so good and open, Daddy," the thick fog of subspace coating his words.

"Thank you for telling me. For right now, though, Daddy's gonna to need to take a break. We had a bit of a Situation and I'm feeling a little shaky."

"Okay, Daddy." He paused. "Did you lose the plug in me?"

"Yes, but I got it out."

"Oh, good."

He slid his knees backward until he was flat on his stomach. Once he had settled into a comfortable position, I let my body start to relax, and curl up against him. Gently, I let my fingers graze his back while I tried to calm my heartbeat down to a less dizzying pace.

"You okay, Daddy?"

I took a deep breath and let it out before I answered.

"Yes, I didn't want to harm you and super don't want to deal with the ER during a pandammit. Now I'm just tired."

He giggled into my chest at "pandammit" and I felt myself relax a little more. And yet, I hugged him harder.

"I'm okay, Daddy. We can just rest. Like you tell me, it's okay to rest."

"You're such a good boy, did you know that?"

"I try."

"And you succeed."

I centered myself in the bed and the warmth of his body and reminded myself that he's okay, and that I *might* not be the worst Daddy ever. I was trying not to chide myself that I should've known better with that joke of a flange on the plug. The spicy scent of his Darkfall cologne, mingled with sex, filled my nose with a little more calm, but I still felt shaky. Unsure.

And very, very weary. I didn't want to disappoint him by ending the scene before either of us had cum, but I just ... couldn't do more at that moment. I remembered what I learned from *my* Daddy, when I'd had one. That it was okay for Daddies to have limits, too.

As I listened to my boy's regular breath, the rhythmic rise and fall, I started drifting towards sleep. I could feel him melting into a nap in my arms, also, furthering my relief.

*He was safe. It was okay. He was safe. It was okay.*

I repeated this mantra until sleep overtook me. I don't remember dreaming, but once I opened my eyes again, I saw his big, sparkling eyes looking up at me. The horniness in them was unmistakable, but so was the restraint. He was trying to read my energy and whether or not I woke up ready to play more.

"Mmmmm, well, hello there, my sweet boy," I murmured, my lips curving up just slightly at the edges. I decided to take the question out of his eyes and let my hand drift from his back to between his legs, with some haste, to surprise him a little. When he felt my fingers probing into the pooling wetness surrounding his thick, hard clit, his back arched and he parted his thighs to give me better access to all of him.

"Hi, Daddy," he said in that fucking *voice* that was both sweet and heat and almost never failed to make my cunt clench with need.

Fuck napping more. I needed him. Now.

I lowered my lips to his ear and whispered, "Daddy's going to take you, my boy. Hard. Put your ass in the air, face down."

He gasped and quickly arranged his body in the position I ordered, with only the smallest of whimpers in the process. I looked forward to making more of those sounds come out of him, to pull the screams out of him. Clearly, I was ready to go again.

I reached over to the bedside table where our assortment of cocks were all hanging out with each other, in a glorious phallic rainbow. I picked up his thin green cock and my large purple one and put those between his knees. The addition of anal lube and coconut oil rounded out my happy pile. I knelt behind him and lubed up the green cock.

"Spread your ass like a good whore if you want Daddy to fuck it." There was no softness in my voice anymore.

He quickly did as he was told. I stared at his tightly puckered asshole for a moment, making sure there was no damage. The skin wasn't inflamed nor abraded, thankfully. I didn't think it would be since I had lubed him to heaven and back before. There was still a lake of lube remaining, making his hole glisten for me. I grinned and pressed the slender cock to his asshole. It took a bit of firm pressure to get the soft silicone head in, but once it was past his tight sphincter, it was much easier to gently slide in an inch. I felt my boy's moan throughout his body and pushed in a little bit further.

"That's my good whore...."

"Yes, oh Daddy yes. Fill my whore ass, please."

"Oh, I will. And you know what else I'm going to do once I get it in there?"

Silence.

"I'm going to fill your filthy pussy, too."

"That's too much, Daddy. I can't fit all that."

"Oh, I know you can, my boy. I've fucked both your holes before. You might be a little tight, but I know you can take it for Daddy."

"Daddy, it's so much. Oh, FUCK," he protested as I pushed the last two inches of the green cock into his ass.

"Hold that there, slut."

Again he did as he was told, but this time, the whimper was longer, louder, and more whiny. But his cunt was a veritable fountain too, clenching, dripping, needing to be filled. I grabbed my thick purple dick and rubbed the head up and down his pussy, getting it good and coated in juicy wetness.

"Ready, my boy?"

"Daddy!!!"

"Now my boy; One, 'Daddy' isn't your safeword," I stated very clearly while positioning the head against the opening of his sopping wet lips while his hips reared back to meet it. "Two, how are my friends going to use you properly if you can't take two cocks at once? I need to stretch out these holes so you can be Daddy's proper whore. You do still want my friends to come take you like we talked about, don't you my dirty slut?"

There was a pause and I held the head of the toy where it was.

"Yes, please, Daddy. Please, I need your friends to take my holes."

"Good slut," I crooned as I pushed the giant purple cock steadily into his pussy. He screamed as it filled him up to the hilt. Once it did, I didn't pause anymore. I moved his hand from the green cock that he dutifully still held, and began fucking him slow and smooth with both cocks at once.

"Oh fuck, Daddy it's so much, oh fuuuuuuck!"

Once I could feel both his holes opening for me, I moved behind him so my pubic mound was pushing the bigger cock inside his pussy, still keeping the right hand fucking the green cock into his ass. Once I was in position, I switched to the pace I know he loves best: hard, fast, and deep.

The sounds coming out of him were no longer words, but moaning and grunting as he pushed his hips back into mine to meet my thrusts.

"That's right, my boy. That's right, take Daddy's cocks, just like my friends are going to take you. Whichever. Holes. They. Want," I grunted, each thrust emphasizing a word.

"Daddy, can I cum? Please, Daddy…" he gasped and I could feel his body starting to twitch under me. I held onto his hip with my free hand and growled out, "Beg me, boy."

"Please, Daddy, please, please, please….I'm so close, please…"

"Cum." I ordered while keeping my hips going at the punishing speed he so enjoys, feeling his body cross the threshold into wild abandon. His legs started shaking, his body writhing with the intensity of the orgasm rolling off him. I breathed in the wave of energetic pleasure as it crested and crashed into me. His cunt tightened on my cock, making it harder to thrust. Finally, he went limp and I ceased, laying my free hand gently on the small of his back. A grounding reassurance to help him find his way back from the edge when he was ready. After a few moments of ragged breathing, he found his voice.

"Daddy?"

"Yes, my sweet boy?" I cooed gently.

"Can you take the cocks out now? And say nice things to me?" His words were slow and thick now, like he had a mouth full of cotton and bliss.

"Of course, my love. I'm going to take the one out of your ass first, okay? Take a deep breath and… exhale." He did as he was told and I eased it out and laid it on the chux beneath us, while stroking his lower back.

"That's my good, sweet boy. You did so well for Daddy. I'm very proud of you. Taking both of Daddy's cocks at once." He let out a little whimper as his body began to melt downward toward the bed, legs still splayed.

"Okay, my boy. You know your pussy clenches a bit after you cum, so I need you to take a really deep breath…" He did so. "And then let it out." As he breathed in, I pushed the cock in just a fraction and as he exhaled, I firmly and steadily tried to pull it out. His cunt had other plans, though.

"You may want it out, my sweet love, but your pussy seems to have other plans." I noted with a wry grin.

"Guh…"

"My poor spent boy. I need you to take one more deep breath for me," again he did so, but this time I could feel his weariness. "And let it out." Again with the firm, steady pull and this time it shot out and slipped from my hand to land with a sticky silicone bonk on top of the green cock. His body went limp once it was out. I stretched out by his side to hold him, one arm around his back and tightly hooking my leg over his.

"Such a good boy. I'm so proud of you and I love you so much."

I felt his energy relaxing, shifting from tightly coiled to floating on the afterglow of release.

"We're gonna get you some water soon, okay, my boy? Need to keep my slut hydrated."

"Mmmmhmmmm. Yes, Daddy," he murmured, snuggling limply against me.

"And after we do that, we're throwing that fucking plug in the trash."

# A Natural Blessing

Taneeka L. Wilder

As the sky ladles warm, delicious rain,
drops of your perspiration handcuff themselves to my mango flesh.
As birds chirp lovingly off-key,
you hum orgasmic hymns in my ear.
Your crimson tongue, warm and cinnamon toasty,
runs ballerina laps across the base of my neck.
You are Celestial Seasonings,
unbleached Yogi tea bags of chamomile relaxation.
With your tease, you water my nipples with your hot saliva,
drenching your fevered lust into the folds of my navel.
My blouse floweth over,
I am Hellfire breathing smoky orgasms at twilight,
I swivel,
I convulse,
you lap up my vanilla soft serve with the hunger of a lion deprived of its prey.
My cum runneth over.
My body begins to smolder,
desire escalating effervescently into the galaxy of your bones,
I clutch your Soul,
locking it into mine, while blindfolded against a bed of magnolias.
You gargle my travesties,

inserting a finger into my burning lair,
I scream your name,
as your fingers plunge even deeper into my dark, hairy portal,
I replenish you with my Vitamin V for vitality,
providing immunity for every trial and insecurity.
I need more of you, as your tongue darts in and out of my piping mouth pit.
We dance together,
you squeeze my erect nipples through sheer cloth,
you bite them with delicate urgency,
your nails sliver like a snake down the slope of my back.
You moan bird hymns as I meet you in harmony,
I do not see you,
blindfold still in place,
but I feel you with all of my five senses.
Our intimacy, interlocked,
pheromones rising into the ethers,
synergy uniting,
we collide,
we collapse against magnolia trees,
copulating with nature,
as nature,
burning like supernovas in this forest of exploration,
burning brightly into each other, burning brightly for each other.
As the moon gives us its middle finger in envy,
in seething jealousy,
under the guise of a twilight sky,
elemental, forest combustion,
emitting waves of unbridled passion.

# The Kiss

## Titus Androgynous

She kissed her. Hard. On the mouth. She kissed her. Without hesitating. Well ... that's not exactly true. She had been trying all night *not* to kiss her. She had managed not to kiss her in the used bookstore, on the second floor, bathed in the sweet, dry smell of old, warm paper and dust. (What was it that made it smell sweet?) She'd come close, she thought, to kissing her, but there had been other people around. Strangers. She'd looked at her, intensely, longingly, with an ache that grew from her stomach or solar plexus, wherever that place is that hurts in such an intoxicating way. They'd pointed out books to each other. Familiar titles. New ones, too. And they'd leaned against each other, breathing each other's air. They'd bought some books. It felt good to do something, complete a transaction. Regular people do this, right? They come into a store and they look at books and they buy them. See? Normal.

They had left the store and walked hand-in-hand to a restaurant, hands changing position, touching different parts of the palm, the fingers, restless caressing. She hadn't kissed her at dinner, either. There had been a table between them, so that made it easier. They'd talked and played with each other's fingers and eaten and finally left.

She also didn't kiss her on the way home. Neither on the subway nor on the streetcar. She'd felt so strong. Verging on giving in, but not. She had decided ahead of time that she would not be the one to kiss her. She would not initiate. But she would be happy to receive. And all of those looks at the bookstore and across plates at dinner had been willing her—her what? her friend?—to do it.

Then they were home. Alone. She'd busied herself with a few things, turning on lights, putting away groceries. But then she'd looked at her. And then she was kissing her. Just like that.

She must have crossed the floor to get to her. Two, maybe three steps, but she couldn't remember doing it. There was just where she had been before and then here, with her mouth on hers. She hadn't planned it. If she had, she would have made sure, at the very least, that she had finished chewing and swallowing the pecans that she had popped into her mouth the minute before. She didn't know now whether to ignore them, or try subtly to swallow them and then she forgot about them as she was once again overwhelmed with the need for her.

Their mouths opened. She gently bit the other's bottom lip, then dipped her tongue into her mouth. She met a tongue coming the other way. They played, one tongue dominating, the other submitting and then switching, testing. More lip biting and sudden intakes of breath. And then she thought about her hands. Up behind her neck, in her hair, then softly running her thumb along her cheekbone, her throat.

If someone had asked her how it had happened, how she had gone from vowing not to kiss her to kissing her, she would not have had a logical answer. It would have sounded laughable and science-fictiony. She had simply known that there was no future beyond that singular moment that did not include this kiss. Perhaps with this kiss she had saved the universe. Or some form of lower organism, an endangered butterfly maybe or a bacterium had been kept from extinction. That was how she felt.

It was slowing down now. Tongues less fervent, the urgency passing. Shorter kisses like the end of a round of applause. Distinct. Percussive.

Then it was over and they turned from each other, actually walked several paces away from each other to compose themselves, adjust to this new state.

Then their eyes met in this new world, after the kiss.

# And

## Foxhaven

Afterwards, as we lay on the floor in a tumbled mess of naked hands and thighs and bellies and breasts and arms and backs and lips and cunts, I look at the ceiling and think, *There now, see? She really did.* In spite of all the signals and signs, why can I never quite believe that I'm the one they want? *Just take a chance sometimes. Look where it leads you.*

***

It's late enough, and we've drunk just enough, and all night we've been telling stories and laughing. The dinner party, now dwindled down to just the three of us. If there's a sparkle in her eyes every time she looks at me, what of it? She enjoys my company, that's all. That secret smile she gets when she stops talking and looks down? It's for some private memory she doesn't share, or something she doesn't yet want to say. *To me?* And just what is it, *what*? Would she still look at me that way if she knew how many times I've stopped myself from reaching out to touch her? *She's straight, she doesn't want you that way; don't be a fool.* We've finished the food and poured another drink. We beg and we beg and finally the other of us agrees to get up and perform, just a song or two.

A hush comes over the room. She sighs in anticipation. I decide to take a chance. I reach out to put my arm around her and say, "Come here now." She doesn't say no. She squirms her way in closer, leans into and against me. My arm is on her shoulders, and my breast is pressed upon her arm, and she slides just a little further down until her head rests on my shoulder.

I can feel her shiver as she breathes; feel her both sinking into and holding herself back from me. Her eyes are fixed straight ahead. Yes, straight ahead, looking at the singer. Yes, the singer, both handsome and sweet. And I think, *Ah no, I see. This is for them, not for me.*

It's not for me, but them—this racing pulse, the heart so loudly pounding. It's for the singer who opens their lips and sings with a voice that rises right up above your fears and insecurities, then dives and sinks straight into your heart. An old song, a sad, hopeful song. Is it in English or French? No matter, the meaning is clear. You can read it on the singer's face. Her eyes are fixed on them, and her breathing becomes both deeper and quick. I try to peek down at her face, but there's only the top of her head. I can't see her eyes. So instead I strengthen my grip on her shoulder and pull her tighter to me for a moment. She does not resist, but is both pliable and stiff. Both wants and doesn't? Both thrilled and hesitant? I've never held her so intimately before. Nor this long, nor this close.

It's late enough and we're drunk enough. Not too much, just enough.

Now in the song, the singer's lover has left, in spite of all their fierce pleading. And we've applauded, and whooped, and taken more sips of our drinks. And still she does not pull away. In fact, it seems, she has actually moved as little as possible, so as not to dislodge her place.

*She is only cold*, I think, *enjoying the warmth.*

The music starts again, and the singer steps forward. This song a little more aggressive, insistent, but filled with longing and loneliness. I look straight ahead, yes, eyes straight ahead.

The singer catches my eye, holds my gaze, as they thrust out their chest and grab at their crotch in the song. And I think, *Ah yes, just what would they do?*

If I dare to move my other hand, what then? If I put down this glass, wipe off the condensation, and place my other hand on her as well? The singer sings of drinking, and my other hand is on her arm. Hands: one on a shoulder and one on an arm. She nestles her head into me, takes a sip, and puts her hand over mine. Deliberately? Absent-mindedly? Before I can decide, she pulls it back, applauding for the singer, whose song is sung. And I applaud, too, though one-handed, on my thigh, afraid to take my arm from around her; that in doing so, the spell will be broken. She might shift; she might move away.

The crescendo of the song is still sparking in the air. "Another. Another!" I cry. "Encore. Encore!" she echoes. The singer acquiesces, bows, inclines their head, looks me in the eye, and smiles a smile that tells me they know exactly what's going on. I flush. They turn their eyes and smile to her. *Ah damn,* I think, *she's theirs.* They could have her in a moment, if they wanted to. Such talent, such power in this little room, for an audience of two. How could the spell not be woven?

"What would you like?" the singer poses. Neither she nor I know how to answer. "A sad song? A love song? A ballad? A ditty?" *Something long with at least forty stanzas*, I think. "A fun song," she says. "Something to make us smile."

The singer turns aside to select some music. I place my hand back on her arm where it had been, but she's shifted. My hand falls on her arm, yes, but higher now. My knuckles brush along her side. The side of her breast. I feel her breathe in, expect her to move. I'm ready to apologize, "I never meant—" But she once more places her hand over mine, and in doing so pushes my knuckles more firmly into her. The softness of the cup of her bra. The firmer softness underneath.

The singer turns towards us. I see an eyebrow raise, a clocking of our subtly changed positions. The song begins. The girl that never comes, the eternally hopeful suitor. The girl that never comes, the girl… that never … comes. I roll it around in my brain, the meaning shifting, innocent to deep. And I wonder, *And this girl?* And this girl. Could I make her come? Would she like me to?

I hear it inside of me, yes. It resonates inside of me, yes. I realize I've been hearing it all along, this yes. Ever since this woman and I had met. Yes, yes. Is it hers, this yes? Is it mine? Wishful thinking, or wish fulfillment? And the singer sings, "Yes!" And I whisper in her ear now, "Yes?" And she replies, soft and low, "Oh yes. Yes."

And so I uncurl my fingers. And so I am cupping her breast, and she sighs a little "Oh!" and the singer smiles a wolf grin, but keeps singing. I keep on as well.

I move my hand down and pluck at the hem of her shirt. Experimentally. Impatient. Her hand has followed mine and when she knows what I'm after, she pulls up the edge of her shirt just enough so my fingers slide under it. Soon I am touching her flesh. She is all goosebumps. I slip my hand back and forth across her belly, back and forth, back and forth. And each time I do, I inch my little finger down just a little lower. She leans in so I can touch more of her and at last my little finger slides below her waistband.

All along we've been looking at the singer, our eyes straight ahead at them. As their song ends and the next one begins, we don't applaud. We can't move beyond what we're doing, half-frozen with desire for what we've awoken. Afraid one false move will break it.

The singer grabs a chair and sits down. Sitting, they start singing the next song for us. Something voluptuous and slow.

They are watching us intently, and I feel both them and her say: Go on.

I pull my pinky back and forth inside her waistband. She moans and presses closer to me. I try to get more of my hand in, but her trousers are just too tight. I'm about to give up and try a different tack when she reaches over and undoes her button and fly.

Up there in front of us the singer does the same. As I maneuver my hand down further, the singer does the same, moving their own hand down inside their own trousers. Further. As I begin to go on and find what it is I've been looking for, what I've been yearning to touch, the singer matches me move for move.

My fingers find a wetness, and—a soft swollen wetness, and—she arches her head back then, and—thrusts her hips forward, and—

The singer is no longer singing.

I'm looking at *them*, but feeling *her* and I'm teasing and thrusting and finding her clit with my thumb and the singer groans and breathes as our hands move and she moans and breathes as it rises and the three of us are gasping together. It's coming on quickly and soon the singer throws their head back and "Ungh," and she throws her head back and "God," and I grind my teeth and "Mmnn." And. In that moment, the three of us are one.

She lies back panting in my arms. The singer looks at me and smiles, well-satisfied. I smile back and then realize, we've never even kissed. And so I lean down and kiss her. Then call the singer over and kiss them.

And then, we all three of us kiss.

And then, it all starts again.

# Verdean Waves

Ellen Webre

Belts of silver  swing

        around rosy hips,

see how they shift in bangle swirls,

        rivershine in its gunmetal blue.

If you seek to lay          your kisses

        in dips                    of bone,

warm flesh        soft   invitation,

        take her hands in yours,

lips in pilgrim's prayer.          Lay her down,

        splayed butterfly of burgundy velvet.

Roll down        sheer stockings,

        for she is black sugar,

gold sand     sun-kissed nectar          for your tongue.

Take her gently                    by the throat,

    by her curls,                    by her hitched

breath          sigh,          and spread the universe
panting     at her feet.

    Right here.          Right now.

# Write A Letter

Beaux Neal

Fly it over the barbed wire
of the school building. Over-fluffed with itself.

To a plane beyond recess and right doing.
The air, really. A trampoline or an inkling.

When a warm cookie splits in a commercial
it's you again. The con artist's language
is glitter for the eyelids, spread with your soft hands
in granulated sugar weather. Baby powder.

I love it when you walk out
and don't look back.
You were never more attractive
than your own analysis.
Another girl left a valentine on my desk.
Your laugh was the loudest.

Of what nucleus was this. Of what label in your mother's
kitchen.
Of what wall in the suburban quandary
we could knock out just one brick.
Of what a heap and Heathcliff we were, what a phantom mess.

Two noodled pool cues
in the time zone zombie.

You'd come back to me
in humidity, in the word for lazy,
in a sea of iris-less faces.
Brain on a wire.
Hardly here. Online again.

I'm only certain that I can't
find the switch.

You could write a letter, but
I wouldn't know where to open it.

# OCTAVIA

Brenda S. Tolian

I burned the witch
pyre on the mountain
salt sprinkled in her eyes
and hid in the delta of Venus

a crescent
tight and close
a river where water
baptisms are said
to be sacred
she and I
came together

curving fingers
magnolia tangled hair
that sways in the dark water
wrapping like hyacinth vine

afraid when I met her
she was dripping wild cypress
roots below wet dirt
shameless in her form

she gathers Spanish moss
braiding gris-gris
and wraps it twice around
my crown

# Preview

## Leah Rogin

*"I had the radio on."*
*–Marilyn, in a* Time Magazine *interview, when asked if it was true that she had nothing on when posing for the infamous calendar shoot. The photos were eventually purchased by Hugh Hefner for Playboy's first issue.*

Born Norma Jeane Mortenson, baptized Norma Jean Baker, Norma Jean Dougherty when she first married, a few days after her 16th birthday. Mona Monroe posing for nude photos and signing on the dotted line to be paid, before her career had really begun. Zelda Zonk in a brunette wig, traveling incognito, staying at fancy hotels, waiting for her lovers in a white bathrobe. Miss Faye Miller throwing the press off her trail as she signed herself into the psychiatric wing of New York Hospital. Marilyn Monroe Miller (MMM) when she died, the triple MMM initialed doodles outlasting her final marriage.

I ran through all of Norma Jeane's names, thinking about the difference in the way your mouth opens wide and friendly to say "Norma" versus the way your lips close in on themselves and press together, with the slightest hum when you say "Marilyn," which is similar to what your mouth does when you say, "Miriam," my name, except you begin and end on that lip-touching hum.

I remember studying her, understanding that she and Barbie were trying to tell me something.

"She's like a doll," I told my dad, "You think she's beautiful?" I asked.

"I think she's sexy," he replied, then looked embarrassed, as if the word had slipped out, which made it seem important.

I spent a lot of subsequent years holding *beautiful* next to *sexy* to understand the differences.

I thought Madonna and Marilyn were the same lady. It was the '80s, and Madonna was working the Blonde Ambition phase, and she even had a matching-Marilyn beauty mark sometimes. Like Madonna, I came of age with MTV. I was probably too young to be watching "Like a Virgin," but no one really understood music videos yet, and they were too fascinating to turn off.

"Marilyn sure can sing!" I told my dad.

He laughed. "That's Madonna, and she can sing way better than Marilyn," he said.

I watched Madonna's dance moves, comparing "Material Girl" to "Gentlemen Prefer Blondes." Everything about Marilyn was softer than Madonna, I could see that now—her body, her voice, the way she moved.

My father preferred the softness, I guessed. But I liked the way Madonna was hard. I liked that my dad blushed when I asked him what "Papa Don't Preach" was about.

I wanted to be hard so I spent my teenage years in the early '90s trying. Nirvana, grunge, even Madonna fully embraced S&M in those years. I was in good company.

It wasn't until I moved out and went to college that I remembered Marilyn. I was trying to buy my dad a birthday present, and I was in a thrift store, paging through a bin with back issues of *Life Magazine* to find one that coincided with his birth month, and there she was. The Golden Dream.

The cover read December, 1953, *Playboy* #1 and Marilyn waved, clothed, but inside she was laid out across the red velvet, looking as sweet and soft as a bonbon, her nipples cherried in profile. For a nude spread, fairly chaste. Innocent compared to Madonna's newly released book *Sex*, but probably shocking for the '50s.

I slipped the #1 *Playboy* inside a *Life Magazine* from the same year and waved it *Life* side out at the cashier, slid a quarter across the counter.

I went home and inspected these photos. She looked so young and beautiful, a little lost but also completely in control of the page. I kept flipping through her spread, back and forth, looking carefully to see if that was an actual nipple or just the shadow of a nipple. I held her above my head and wondered how many men, how many women, how many people, had inspected her the same way I was doing. I felt shame, but I was so aroused, I couldn't help letting my hand travel between my legs, joining an international club I had never known existed, people around the world, spanning decades, touching themselves while imagining their faces buried between Marilyn's perfectly round breasts.

That was the day my true obsession with Marilyn started. I needed to announce it to someone, this feeling I had about a woman who had already been dead for almost half a century. I called my father.

"You know she never posed for those photos, never even got paid for them, right?" my dad told me when I asked if he'd ever seen the *Playboy*.

"What do you mean? I looked at the photos, Dad. She obviously posed."

"She never posed for *Playboy*. I read she was only paid $50 for some calendar pin-up before she was even a movie star. They sold it to *Playboy* without her permission."

I looked at the cover again, wondering how she felt, taking those nude photos when she was so young, then having them follow her throughout her life.

Years after that, when the announcement about Hugh Hefner's death popped up on my Facebook feed, I thought about that conversation with Dad, how he had mentioned the photos lightly, like a joke, while I immediately understood that it was a story about every woman, everywhere, whose brilliance had only been used to reflect on a man, whose compensation had never been enough.

# Manifest

Lou Stonefruit

I manifest me
in daydreams
Her: with the wild grace
who fucks on a roof in the rain
Cooks enough to feed her whole neighborhood
and still has time to read, for baths
for peace
This me
grows her own food, cans
ferments
She goes to galleries
throws pottery
Doesn't care if her nipples show through her shirt

I have two dreams
two moons bathing me
in their light
Two tides pulling me into
two oceans
two desires
and only one me

in daydreams
on paper

when I plant seeds
when I fuck me
I manifest the me I want to be

# Ride Free

Sarah LaRue

I squirm in my seat
flying
solo southbound on 25
humming
a rented CD Buddhist
teaches friendship with yourself

my left hand wraps
gripping
the wheel while my right hand
—oh my right hand
spreads out straddles my thigh
slow now sliding up
easing
down between snug jeans
warmful belly
tugging buttons
moaning free

fingers spread
searching
meeting
skin softer than skin

my most familiar hiding place

arriving
in departures
rapture widens
swirling hips expand
wilder than within
apartment walls
no neighbors here to stifle my

OH—
my lips
let out a moan
so low
so slow at 90
miles an hour
I hear it as I come in waves
my eyes never leaving the road

as I try on relentless self-love

# Roadside #5, CO 160

Cleo Black

meandering down
curvy mountain pass—
your hand in the air,
elbow on console—
those two fingers
trace the air,
beckon for me

and I clench tight,
writhe there in the seat,
each motion electrifying the air,
flickering through my cells—
this palpable non-touch,
these desperate moans—
you feel what you're doing to me

then the swift turn
into gravelly rock-pocked pull-off,
you perch us over a peaked vista
and come around
to slide up the romper leg,
dive deep inside me

I hang out the door frame,
panting, shuddering, begging,
and my tongue seeks yours
to ground us in familiar stimulation
as you take me up
into the atmosphere
far above the clouds I see,
beyond the beyond

splayed open,
my face goes slack,
all control lost,
I have come undone.
we merge into this conversation
between your hand
and my pussy—
they dance,
unencumbered by thought

everything is buzzing
with this vibration,
this longing

and my hand now
forages for honey,
goes spelunking
in that sweet, dank cave
so that your gasps
syncopate my moans,
and we are weaving
motion into sound
in this valley overlook
outside of time

and the cool mountain breeze
rustles up and through
from the depths of the canyon,
and this energy spirals
into immeasurable releases
from the depths of my body,
and we cling to this force
as it overpowers reason.

We whisper "I love you"
because it tries to encompass
this power we feel,
but can we ever pinpoint
just how
we made the world stop spinning?

# Snow Squall

Oliver Antoni Krawczyk

An unwavering wrath. A splooge
snow shot. A sneezing snot
blot. Fifteen minutes melt
into the tongue of time:
A layer of snow firm
on the hard ground.

The dark sky is lit with
pollution. It's so radiating,
so bright. It seeks you in,
draws every drop of blood out.
The clouds swell under
the sharp relief of it.

The squall is the flick of wind
a hooded clit. A silly tongue. A barred tarot spread
gripping unwanted truths. Unrevealed
in clouded night, revel in the chill.

Touch what skin you can. Freeze
and thaw until I'm crisp
and burnt.

O squall splendor release me
for nothing we're all worth
which is everything.

# amassing fire signs, I must be preparing for the end of something

Emily Duffy

Here lies a dried flower
Cotton splayed out like an angel
Caught in brambles where I
Took out my tampon to fuck

Karst juts out from the ground in the most unexpected places
You held up my duster so I could piss privately
Beside a tree in a residential neighborhood
Picked me a flower
Called me an angel
Bent your knees to concrete to taste me

Buried each piece of my throbbing heart
And watered, and water, and water
Reptilian girl with eyes that move back and forth
So pissed to be socialized as prey
So clearly a predator why did you have to wait until the other side of twenty-five to
Learn how sharp your talons
Imagine this a watercolor: my sleeping face between your thighs

With every speculative gesture
The universe puts me in your path again
And I am looping in that moment when I saw you smoking
against a column and asked for the first time
If you had fire

# Fire

Orlando Silver

The flare of lightning splits the night sky. I see you, the edges of you, lit in silver and bound in steel, the hardness of your body that I am devoted to.

Folks might name me a butch dyke, if they wanted to. I try not to give myself names because moment-by-moment, things change. My old lover called me a butch dyke, but in bed called me Sir, and that suited me plenty. I'm a woman, but I take the things that men think they're entitled to and make them my own. I guess that's what revolution looks like.

You were coming back from the dark place, near the tents. In a minute, Lexi would arrive too, shamefaced and blushing. We all knew you had a thing going.

You were laughing as you walked. I could hear your voice over the rough peals of thunder.

"We should really move," you are saying, but none of us is going anywhere, standing by the raging fire we had built out here in the middle of nowhere. We had dragged huge logs through undergrowth for this very reason.

Sam had spent time twisting paper into firelighters. Little twigs and more and more until this, where the fire in the clearing burned as high as a man.

It was dangerous and stupid but something in us, all of us, needed the vast energy. We did it wordlessly. We were here to play, all of us, unwitnessed.

The eucalyptus rustled in the thrilling night breeze, feeling the air shift. The winds grew.

I sat on the stump and watched the way you kissed your friends, your sweet mouth moving against cheeks. The spark in your heart visible as you leant your affections to anyone but me.

Again, the lightning, and the forks of swift light that pushed through the air finally did something to my heart.

I would let you go, I decided. I would let you go, how could I persist like this. For months I had sought you, watched you and waited for you to notice. You wouldn't and you won't.

I looked down and saw my old boots, the threaded laces, the soft grass underneath. I breathed out.

But when I looked up you were there, next to me, standing with your back to flames.

"Hi," you said and I said nothing and you smiled. I said nothing because my whole body suddenly filled with hope and longing like a magnet, and you tilted your body so that your hips became sharp and I knew with certainty then I loved you.

It was a fishhook in my heart, and I loved you. Fucking goddamn.

I sat back and gave you my full attention, like we were already lovers.

"I can never read you," you said.

"That's good," I said, letting my body be soft. Letting you see that I would not give away anything that easily. Letting you see that you should work for me, if you want it.

The blade my father got is hanging loose on my waist and I see you looking. I see you witnessing the way the old leather of the sheath is well-handled and soft. This is not a performative tool, like the leather the new kids wear to the gay men's night. This is worn in. This is well used.

This is what you want.

"Where's Lexi?" I ask, and watch the blush rise.

"Oh, somewhere," you say, attempting a casual tone. You sit then, at my feet, which charms me absolutely.

The large clouds make the night seem darker, but you are close to the flames and I can see little beads of sweat are on your brow.

"Come," I gesture, and put you between my legs, facing the fire. So I can rub your back. I use my large hands to expertly work at you. I do your neck. I do the span of your shoulders. I use strong fingers around the base of your skull.

People start watching, and I feel good about it. Everyone likes to see a firefly tamed. You start feeling soft in my hands, surrendered, and then there are little moans that only I can hear. You murmur my name and my cunt feels electric with it.

I will have more of that, I think.

One hand holding the scruff of your neck, I use the other to dip my hand down the front of your shirt, in front of everyone, kneading your small, handsome breasts. You shudder and groan but do not squirm. Your eyes are closed now.

"Good girl," I murmur, breathing into your ear. "I'd like you to give me this please."

You nod, because no words now. No smart alec quips or clever retorts.

I move slow, letting my hands own you.

The lightning again, then thunder almost immediately after. The first fat drops of rain sizzle on the fire and people start getting up.

I make you stay.

"Just a little longer," I say. I don't want to be watched for this last part.

People disappear in couples, or in threes, moving into darkness to play or talk or love each other. There are plenty of glances at you. At me. There are plenty of people who would like to help, but I keep my eyes low.

I want you to myself and I offer no invitation.

The rain begins, a slow pelting rhythm. I want all the sensation on you as I lift you up and make you straddle me. You are grinding now, a little helplessly, and I think with pleasure about what I will do.

The fire still burns big behind us. I want this image forever, with you on my lap, riding me, feeling for the knife on my belt and begging me. Me with strong hands holding you down and bruising your hips.

The thunder sounds, hard and fierce above our heads. I take my knife and carefully, with ease, slice the little shirt you are wearing down the middle. I see the blade gleam in the fire. I see the glint in your eye.

Yes. Give me those fierce edges then, my love.

You steady, instantly, breathing deep. I pull you to me. I call you in. The rain makes soft rivers over your breasts and I drink heavily, the crystal water offering me everything I wanted. I lick your taut nipples, your goosebumped skin, the ridges of your clavicles.

Then, in a quick movement I sheath my knife and stand, lifting you with one hand to the ground.

I gesture to my tent on the far side of the clearing. You nod.

"Yes," you breathe, the orange-red light of the fire still spreading across your skin.

"I'm ready."

# Mattress

Kat Sanford

Late in the night I take an x-acto knife and punch a small
hole in the mattress.
I carve a piece about the size of my palm,
peel it loose from the soil of sleep and gently fold it into my
mouth.

The chewing is difficult and slow.
Some of the pieces taste like nothing special,
sometimes it is like you were never here at all.
But some still hold your mouth as real as if I were biting your
lips.

When I finish, I cover it back up with the fitted cotton sheet.
I do this every night.

I will swallow every inch of this mattress,
every left-behind skin cell and hangnail,
each drop of dried sweat, all the tiny tangled hairs.

Nobody has noticed the slow change in the shape of the bed,
but they keep commenting on how much more slender my
body is.
I can't tell them that the only thing I want to eat anymore
is you.

My gut rots on fibers that once held your sleeping body and I am so fucking hungry.

When I was 14, I watched my father eat bird's nest soup and I thought,
each bite used to cradle a delicate baby swiftlet.
Why would anybody want to eat that?

The first bite, the night after you left, tasted exactly like your shoulder.
I wrapped my teeth around it as if it were real, as if it were your body.
I have consumed you so tenderly.

The last time we fucked, you pressed your face into the corner of the mattress so hard I thought you would stop breathing.
I am saving that bite for last.

# In My Thirties, I Become Obsessed with Werewolves

Liv Mammone

I didn't know I cradled my own monster
Over black and white movie
soundtrack crackle
I didn't hear tendons shredding
Humans rewrote what should have been a mythology of skin
The stories all demand *who will you hurt?*
Not *how were  you hurt?*
This skin is the walls of a plague house
Here are joints transforming
Here is me disappearing to myself
My worst fear is my own body
My body won't do me the kindness of death
Evolution didn't account for this so I am proof of God
which makes me God
I am hard to look at
which makes me God
The planet yanks me forward
it is ripping itself open
The sky is a wall between me and all I was
Stars are pustules
The moon is an infection

Clouds bulge spit and blood.
I inside out empty
I palace of nerve endings
Every month I get less and less human
I look so young!
I am watching the sky
I am chasing the sun
I grind my teeth against the howl
and try not to pee in doorways
Everyone standing upright bates my rage
I eat decay
I'm inside the nursery rhyme
Relegated bad dream
Didn't ask for this
Inside the breaking I have no name no past and no one loves me
Inside the pain love does nothing
There is only the hunger to spread what I am
My teeth will make you understand
I am just on the other side of your good flesh
Can you see your face in the strands of my saliva?
Daylight won't last forever
I wish to infect you all with my unstoppable dying

# An Open Account

Te V. Smith

His wife fucks me on *Hump Day* and he tries to make love to me on Saturdays. She isn't harsh, just restless and hungry. Our text messages and breathy phone conversations are full of angst and suspense. The opposite of her, he is timid and requires coaching. I don't mind. *Coaching* is a soft definition for *dominating*. I handle everything. Keep it simple and routine. Train him.

She anxiously schedules day-rooms the same way a dog (he refers to her as *The Bitch*) attacks affection after being shut up all day. The wife and I rarely frequent the same hotel twice. Overuse of any particular spice makes for a lazy appetite. This week's choice is a 4-star hotel in the heart of the French Quarter. I arrive early, hold a smile with the receptionist whose gaze slides discreetly over my body. I let him graze my palm as he places the second key in my hand.

The room, a charming corner suite, is painted a nude cream with a lush gray rug at the foot of the bed. I insist we always book the first floor, because anything worth having is worth risking: a show for those passing by the open windows and the heightened probability of running into someone she knows on our way out. The sensual discomfort (for her) of holding hands is part of our lovely arrangement.

I sit the gallon of water on top of the mini fridge, pull the candle from my canvas tote bag, light it, and set the thermostat five degrees colder than it should be. I undress slowly in front of the mirror: drape the silk robe (a gift from him) over my shoulders, thrust my arms through, and roll on scented oil. Nothing strong enough to taste. I drag a chair near the window as the sunshine drools from the top of the blinds. I sit. She likes to meet me in the light.

***

It took nearly most of the summer for me to say yes. They had both become regulars at our branch. The Meyers: a svelte blond in an endless series of stylish skirt-and-blouse ensembles with thick hair that fell in waves around her shoulders and a tall, muscular man in uninspiring slacks, thick ties, and shirts that hinted at a subdued strength. Fairly attractive. In their late 40s. Fairly dry. The game was in building suspense: catching their eye and keeping them there past discomfort, drenching them in compliments, and exaggerated greetings as if I'd been missing them all week. The wife withdrew every Wednesday afternoon at 5:00, and he, you guessed it, deposited into their joint account every Saturday morning. After the first month, I noticed her intentional placement in my line. The nervous wandering eyes as she allowed others to pass her in line until I was available.

"You're dangerous," she jokingly whispered through the bottom of the glass opening, one afternoon. "You know exactly what and who I can afford." I smiled as she strutted away, I'm sure satisfied with her rehearsed moment of brevity. The next week she sauntered in wearing a wine-colored skirt that hugged her skin and announced the slim curves of her pilates-body. She waited her turn with her eyes fixed on me. She didn't speak, just smiled and slid her number underneath the withdrawal slip. After our first text, there was a series of yes's: *Coffee?* Yes. *Can you talk for a second?* Yes. *How about a goodnight pic?* Yes.

Her husband wasn't so straightforward. He was more of the—May I contact you if I have questions about my account?—type. An indirect seduction spoken under too much cologne. We sent text messages for weeks. Our first phone call was followed by a series of conversations over coffee during my break or late evenings. His curiosity bordered somewhere between intimacy and interrogation. His fretful aggression took some getting used to, but then, once I accepted it as fumbling foreplay, it became fun, an extension of the game. *What's your favorite Thai dish? How many times have you done this? You won't tell anyone about this, will you?* Tom Yum Goong. Once in college, almost. About what?

***

Wednesday at 2:15, the wife's key slides into the electronic slot. I loosen my robe, push the chair against the wall, and stand. The door opens. Her eyes pace the halls before she quickly enters. Her deep sigh is cut short at the sight of me. I see the gnawing hunger in her eyes. I smirk. I nod, yes. She kicks her leg back to slide off her heels, unzips her black pencil skirt, and lets it fall to the floor. I wave my finger for her to come. She walks over—chest heaving, nipples pressing against her thin blouse—and squats in front of me. She runs her hands up my thighs, around my waist to my ass, dips her head, brings my dick (she likes how the word flicks off the roof of her mouth. *d i c k*) up with her lips, licks the base of my shaft, and slowly massages me into her mouth. I moan and listen. Sound is as important as touch.

After about a minute, I let out a soft roar. I fill my hands with blond hair and pull her slobbering face back. She looks up and grins. I seize her by the chin and stare into her eyes as if I can see right through. She stands to her feet and I push her legs open with my thigh. I drop my hand from her head and grab the back of the shirt I plan to tear off of her soon. She is warm and ready. I slide in two fingers, lift gently, and slowly flick my thumb. She whimpers, stretches her hand around my throat, and gives a gentle squeeze. "You fucking mutt," the wife sighs as

I wag against her, pant, and ignore the moaning text alert from her husband.

***

She was born in a small suburb just outside of St. Louis, Missouri. Her family moved to Philadelphia in the summer of her freshman year of high school. At her parents' encouragement, she earned a law degree from Drexel University, and after years working as in-house counsel, settled in New Orleans to start her own bankruptcy law practice and later became a prominent member of the board of directors for the Greater Faith Center: a mid-level church her husband founded 10 years ago. They share a home in Metairie, Louisiana and a beach house in Florida.

Her husband was born and raised in Denver. Attended seminary in New Orleans where he met his wife during a chance encounter at the retirement party of the former lawyer-turned-writer, Carlos Ruffin. They dated for a year before he proposed during a Bible study. Ceremony at the Benachi House in New Orleans. Honeymoon in St. Lucia. There'd been no time to have children in between tending to a legal practice and a growing church. His congregation knows nothing of the God we worship every Saturday.

Neither does his wife.

***

"You'll have to calm down, if you came to fuck me."

It takes 15 minutes and stern direction for his nerves to settle, for him to stop pacing, babbling prayers, and remember that his purpose here is to be made in *my* image. I walk over and slowly unbutton his exhausted white shirt, unfasten his navy chino pants, and lower them to his ankles with my foot. I remove his thick clear frames and stroke his sparse silver-blond hair as I kiss away his fears. I linger. His mouth is delicate, almost fragile with its thin lips. His stubble beard is soft and smells of citrus cedar and sandalwood. (Moisturization was his homework last week.) The curtains of our fifth-floor suite are drawn modestly. The light is dark and still with brief silhouettes of our bodies, firm and soft, flickering against the walls from the candle I used a month ago with his wife, on the nightstand. I step back until my legs are pressed against the bottom of the bed. He stands helpless before me. "Stop shivering." I say, sharp with a low growl. "I want you lovely."

My pet (that's how she describes her pathologically sensitive husband when I'm half-listening to her complain about their failing marriage) has been trained to crawl forward and warm his cold hands around my erection before he is allowed to touch any more of my body. I smile at the sensation of his graceful hands moving about. He once dreamt of becoming a famous pianist. So, I lean, arch my back, and let my cock (his word of choice) rest in his hands. He tilts his head against my inner thigh and looks up for approval. I nod and bite into my lip. His fingers reach octaves up to my chest. His mouth is ravenous. His finger swirls wildly behind me, inside of me. I am a medley of desires. "Take your time," I moan. I stop him, sit up and gently push him away. I grin, pull him toward me, and turn around. I rest my knees on the edge of the bed and stretch—bend forward and grip the sheets. "Come," I whisper. His left hand grips my waist as he guides himself in me. I reach back and pull his legs closer—pull him deeper into me. His nails claw into my back. We are lurched into a rising crescendo. My entire body is an applause and we are a glorious melody, a fucking Puccini opera.

***

June fifth, at 6:30 in the evening. That's when the novelty of our *thing* officially expired. The husband sends me a message, failing at his attempt to explain why he can no longer see me. Lengthy text messages expressed how much I had helped him rediscover his passion and how that passion reignited his love for his wife—the fire in his marriage. He was sorry, oh so very sorry. He sent Cashapp gifts and then apologized by sending more. He wanted so badly for me to respond, to let him off the hook. I didn't. I remained silent as I read his long reiterative text messages. I typed a letter. Three bubbles. Deleted it for suspense. I repeated twice more, smiled, and placed the phone on the nightstand as his wife lay, napping, next to me.

A month later, a phone call, from her, arrived with a similar tone. Almost identical as if they had been sitting across from one another drafting the pitiful let-me-down-easy script together. She thanked me. She would *never forget what we shared* and assured me her feelings were real: every "I love you" and "I wish we could last here forever" was meant from her soul. She cried, then after paused moments in her hysteria (where I was expected to soothe her), she yelled and demanded that I say something, that I scream at her or cry with her. I couldn't. She was right to end it. Things had gotten stale: awkward hotel-room lunch dates. Rendezvous replaced with phone calls. So much talking. There were much better things to do with our mouths. I placed the phone on the table in my apartment and offered an occasional grunt so she'd believe I was listening. When she had finished, I whispered a soft "thank you" before hanging up.

The Meyers either stopped frequenting or had changed their bank-trips to the days I didn't work. By the end of fall, I'd almost forgotten about the couple. Wednesdays and Saturdays had slid back into their dull calendar slots. At the start of the new year, I was promoted to Relationship Manager and transferred to our branch uptown.

Mr. and Mrs. Brown, a fairly attractive couple in their early fifties, recently relocated to New Orleans, and sat with me last week for a consultation. She has a nice smile. They are coming in today to open an account.

# shatter

## Jessica Lawson

i.
this glass we've made i gather in a basket
you ask me to sand your fingerprints

here is the site of our accident
the ground of it looks wet and cuts
i fold away my letter

to sand your fingerprints from the glass we left
i smooth shard accidents into no more

glass catches light and makes the ground look wet
i take a step and it becomes

our ground becomes wet as it cuts my steps
my letter names into folds the sites to remove
to remove the letters from the page i take steps
making wet the ground that looked it

this glass we've made i gather in a basket
you ask me to catch the light and make nothing wet
nothing wet in the aftermath of fingerprints you ask
you ask me to sand your fingerprints from the glass we left

you ask me as if my feet are not bleeding

to sand your fingerprints from the glass we left
i smooth shard accidents into no more
than tender extended globes

ii.
this basket i've made in an accidental bed
i press the smoothed glass in the woven cradle
her wet body prints my fingers
where she is not you

a body has a wet place that can hold
and when it does not we call it empty
the body's wet place is not even empty
but i am
my emptiness is my best approximation
of being wet without taking
cutting steps along our accident

being empty with smooth sanded glass in hand
is my best approximation of being
wet in her bed where i am not
where my erasers' shed skin disappears
when i reconsider my letters to you

she asked me not to stop i did not
she asked me not to stop i did not stop
she asked me not to stop i did not stop anything
she asked me not to stop i did not stop
anything but my heart which stops
the letters and our shatter
i did not stop wrist deep in a basket

where i gathered the glass we made
glass we made and i made smooth
you asked me to let you stop and i let you stop
everything but my heart
and this mess of shards

i worked her to a froth with the detritus of our accident

this mess of shards
smoothed over and shoved
shoved so deep it knuckled the door in my chest

she asked me not to stop i did not stop
my heart from burning in another room you told me
i was too hot to touch you asked me
to let you stop
before my body made us into
an accident of warmth

iii.
arriving home
from her home
i wash each piece of smooth glass
till its color reappears
i place them one by one in my mouth
swallowing a prayer they might regrow their sharp edges
claw the walls their way down through me
leave a mark somewhere that we happened

you ask me to let you stop you do not want
to hurt me and i want
a record of the temperature that changed us

i clean us up against tender
extended globes my mouth
grabs like i'm falling
i'm falling into my own nostrils
where her smell stays even after
the shower and the shower does me no kindness
water keeping me
on this side of the drain

i love you in the clots that keep
my insides inside
intact or otherwise

i write a poem in an empty pelvic cradle
i blow my print like a lash
making this wish where you have
fingered my heart to sand

# She's Cumming For You

## Stina French

when you cum now
no Inanna, yet you circle
the idea of being sexual again
you flirt with other exes
send tit pics to friends
then flinch, self-suspicious
(*are you a hole to fill*)
your pussy is a blank space you ignore
except for the occasional induced orgasm
you never go inside yourself anymore
you take no pleasure
in your pleasure

she is gone but you have to live here
you teach an erotic writing class
you gaze upon the sea of open smiling faces in the Zoom room
and get so turned on after you start to feel yourself
your hips circle to some music
you feel sexy then you shrink
is this distraction
or presence
you think
is this seeking to feel
or actual feels

you decide to practice
to commit to practice
reading practice
writing practice
movement practice
singing practice
anything to bring you back
your voice coach says practice is flinging
paint at the wall you sing
in the shower where she wrote
Don't Give Up and Never Surrender
the letters have blurred
now they say
   o   Give Up          ever render

you imagine elephants ambling
down a riverbank
trunks curled around tails
as you try to think
and try not to think
about keeping your ribcage lifted
your jaw dropped
the distance between the corners of your mouth
you ponder the nature of surrender
how to let go but not
give up

to get in your mask you get out of the water
go bottom up
thus flipped you find it
you drip all over your face
you rise laughing
fling actual paint at the actual bathroom wall

you can't remember the last time you were so inside yourself
it's freedom in the face of everything
that can falter
(*haven't you eaten your own demons long enough*)

now you're inside Erica Jong's zipless fuck
on the way to the bedroom
tell the dog not to follow
finger your clit before you're even laying down
close your eyes
imagine a woman
her cunt
not your ex girlfriend's
give it uneven fuzz
one lip longer than the other

say I wanna slide my tongue
so slow up your slit
say I wanna split you open
thrill to your voice saying these things
say more things: I'm gonna make your clit so big
before I suck it I want you shaking on my fist
it's working
work your nipples
they feel something
it's been so long since they felt something
hope the dog doesn't come in
turn the vibrator up
say cum for me
I wanna feel you cumming for me

but in that leap
from plateau to peak

you falter
(*are you still here*)
you think of her
and try not to think of her
your own pussy isn't even your own pussy anymore
(*is all of you an exit wound*)
you think you may never enjoy fucking
a woman or yourself
you wonder if you'll ever cum without
wondering if she's cumming

she's not coming
to save you
to put you back in
to tell you you have a right to this

oh give it up
drop it in your own waters
oh love
render you unto you
render unto me what is mine
tell us we have a right to this
(*tell us it's not all our fault*)
listen to our pussy
invite us to have a pussy again
imagine only our own pussy
(*it is an arc   we can come inside*)
move our fingers down
keep the voice stroking
cum for me  I'm so wet now
cum for me  I'm going in

and then and as soon as

like a drop of ink in water
we cum
the sudden spreading of wet inside
wet paying witness
to our own arrival

no one is coming for you
you are coming for you
you are coming
to put you back in

# No More Masters

Aerik Francis

*Pleasure is Black.*
*–Robin Coste Lewis*

how easily the word master–
meaning enslaver—slips into
any word master—meaning
expertise, to control—

bait—to attract prey—
bate—to beat, to blow—
bait—to torment—
bate—to cease

the violence
in association
in etymology—

*manu*—meaning manual, by hand.
*stuprare*—to stupify, defile, disturb–
*masturbate*—

I masturbate against masteries—
*give me no seat at the table*
*let no trembling hands lay*

I masturbate, against systems
sapping spirits numb—I resist
insisting liberation be pleasurable

I masturbate against
the mirror, mimesis of
me, mise en abyme—

I masturbate because
nobody will touch me
how I touch myself—

I masturbate because
it feels good and I want to
remember: I have a body—

*Men masturbate differently*, a quotation that
returns to me often, was said by a friend in
the middle of the circle jerk called
seminar—assumption being repetitive
motion only for the self only the hand the
shaft & the eyes only a small collection of
nerves just enough stimulation to erect the
blood to spill to coax the cum to
erupt—

and I wonder
if I am a man, or what kind
if I am ashamed

ashamed of men
ashamed for men

ashamed
by my fascination
with fascinum—

I wonder how much I'm indoctrinated
by the ubiquity of phallic symbols
made synonymous with domination—

but this too is the force of patriarchy—
forcing invasion to make gender—
forcing sex to make gender—

in truth, I don't want
to penetrate anything
or anyone but me—

I am still learning
who I am & what
my body enjoys
coming to embrace

my floral curiosity
my erotic monoecious
my pistillpenis
my stamenclitoris

people will still believe whatever
they want about my sexuality—
but I don't desire their

stimulation, I desire to be
pleased          and please
I have a whole body—I invite

my thighs to hand job, I invite
my nipples to harden, I invite
my fingers to prostate, I invite

my lungs to orgasm, I invite
my voice to shoot, I press
my belly and push an on button

I press upon any pressure point
to linger I invite my depression
to flow and I ebb and invite my tears

to ejaculate I invite my finishing.
I do not take this for granted:
I *finish.* This is something

completed, brought to climax, an ending
I've quit many times to achieve. Come

celebrate. I complete myself. I finish
and I am different, every time.

# Ode to the Tender Boys

ellie swensson

An ode to the tender boys:
with soft eyes, sharp jaw, and agile tongue.

How you stand on that back wall so well.
How you make poppies of pocketed fists.
How you dip low in shadow and smile shameless come sunrise.
How y'all got my number before you even ask for it.
How you push my depths like a grit salve.
How you slow roll to stride my skin.

You, the rough
touch of hand-cut masculine,
that radical chip
off the toxic block.

Rust.
Velvet.
Brick dust to blade.
Oil swerve and a pressed collar.
The textures of complicated love grown from the soul up.
Respect sung in
reciprocal refrains of
*you do you and you do it so well.*

You, hands too powerful, voice too powerful to ever be taken at face value.
You, making my slut side swoon to bare more than my body.
You, the smooth callus swerve of dirt nail to daddy.
You, the weakness I wear proud and walk tall with.

I know y'all well but am always surprised
how you take my breath endless.

How you belly up with that softness as armor.

I meet you with direct eye contact and sure stepping.
I meet you solicitous in every room where queer is an open call.
I flirt with that certain kind of safety you cradle in your hands.
I lean to you with vigor, wake softened and tended,
and I flex my femme so you know you ain't never alone.

This wild world would take it all from us, tender boys, but I'd build for you always.
Keep you arm's length from the brawl in a way that honors your pride.
Your knuckles kissed
        and bruised.

I'd keep you
as you'd have me.

You, road weary and still willing to burn.
You, tending a dream we were both told ain't for us.
You, standing strong.
You, standing strong against
                that back wall
                that light post

that corner store
that alley,
against that apprehension,
against that patriarchal misuse of chivalry.
You standing in the doorway,
strong, crossed arms and open chest,
strong,
open to the ones you're fighting for.
Loyalty knows no better banner than your mouth to my hand
and how you stand
for me
and you stand for yourself
and you stand
for the kind of good I was raised to say grace about.

I'll say grace for you, tender boys,
for your safe passage,
for rest,
for release,
for the ease of my thumb tracing the soul aperture of your furrowed brow.

An ode of grace, for you.
This is for you.

# Prior Publications

"After the Two-Hour Scene ... " by Sinclair Sexsmith, in *Daddy-4Daddy: Queer Kink Erotica* (Silvertongue Publishing, 2023).

"An Exploration of Plated Passions," by Aida Manduley, in *Queer Poets Write About Nature* (Cutlines Press, 2018).

"Latin Freestyle" by David-Matthew Barnes, in *Crimes Against My Nature* (Blue Dasher Press, 2021).

"Ode To The Tender Boys" by ellie swensson, in *Salt Of Us* (Punch Drunk Press, 2019).

"Preview" by Leah Rogin, in *Burying Norma Jeane* (Blackwater Press, 2024).

"Shatter" by Jessica Lawson, *Paperbag Magazine.*

"The Wife and Her Pastor" by Amanda E.K., excerpted from her erotic story collection, *The Risk it Takes to Bloom* (Glass Cactus, 2024).

# Author Bios

**Andy Izenson** is a wizard, a hedonist, and a transsexual who lives in a queer commune on unceded Lenape/Esopus land in the Hudson Valley. On the clock, Andy can be found providing legal support to nontraditional families and trans community members at the Chosen Family Law Center and fighting for prison abolition with the National Lawyers Guild, and the rest of the time, they write compulsively, sing show tunes poorly, glue rhinestones to things, and desperately miss throwing raucous parties.

**Kel Hardy** is a queer erotica writer living in Toronto's Gay Village. They co-produce Smut Peddlers, a live erotica reading event at Glad Day Bookshop, the world's oldest LGBTQ+ bookstore. They co-edited *Smut Peddlers: Glad Day 50*, which *Cosmopolitan* praised as "totally expanding contemporary erotica." Smut Peddlers was also a finalist for the 2021 Lambda Literary Award for Erotica. In 2021, they published *DARK: a zine of queer BDSM erotica* with Goblin Cat Press. They have also had stories featured in various queer publications and zines. Kel identifies as a white non-binary writer, story-teller, community organizer, and sex nerd. They believe in telling stories that normalize the coexistence of filth and intimacy, kindness and violence, and the radical power of hedonism.

**Ahja Fox** is the Poet Laureate of Aurora, Colorado. She has editorial, hosting, and teaching experience and has published in various online and print journals. One of her two draft manuscripts was a CAAPP Book Prize Finalist in 2021 and a GASHER Press First Book Scholarship Finalist in 2022. Discover more at dangerspoetics.wordpress.com/, and follow her on any social media platform @aefoxx.

**Kit Tara Eret** began writing erotica on a dare with herself to submit a flash piece to Circlet Press. To her amazement, they accepted her story. She subsequently has had several pieces published there, as well as a catalog of self-published works and a few published in *Cliterature Journal*. In addition to erotica, Kit also writes speculative fiction and poetry. When she's not writing, Kit likes to watch Netflix, read, or cuddle with her two cats.

**Aida Manduley** is an award-winning Latinx organizer, trauma-focused therapist, and international presenter/consultant known for big earrings and tackling taboos. Their politics are radical, their play is ridiculous, and their penchant for irreverence as intimacy is notorious. Whether you want to discuss la petite mort or actual death, Aida's jam is tackling pleasure and justice from cradle to grave. Armed with a stash of glitter and nails sharp enough to kill bigots, you may also find Manduley lifting heavy objects, dancing and drumming in unexpected places, running around covered in paint and clay, and working on alternatives to policing/criminalization.

**Rachel Ann Harding** is a traditional storyteller who is passionate about sharing beautiful folk, myth, and traditional tales. In 2018, she was a featured storyteller for the Exchange Place at the National Storytelling Festival in Jonesborough, TN, and in 2022, she received the Oracle Award for Regional Excellence.

She is the creator and producer of the *Story Story Podcast*, which showcases traditional storytelling from around the world. Rachel Ann believes that fairytales are for all ages.

**Kiki DeLovely** is a witchy, kinky, polyamorous, mixed, nonbinary femme who moonlights as an erotica writer when she's not weaving magic through energetic healing and spiritual coaching. Kiki strives toward erotica that reads as fine literature and connects us with our highest selves. Their work has appeared in dozens of publications and they have toured both nationally and internationally, living and traveling all over the world. She now makes her home on unceded Occaneechi-Saponi land.

**Duffy DeMarco,** in the mid-90s, found a home for their words within poetry slams, earnest writing groups, performance poetry, and independent 'zines. Having taken a whole lot of detours since then, they now mostly write musings about sex, love, pain, and self-discovery in the notes app of their phone as they try to juggle being a neurodivergent, single parent, and psych nurse.

**Valentine Sylvester** is a genderqueer writer and amateur radio DJ whose eclectic music show, *The Monster of Love*, broadcasts live on WUVT-FM 90.7 and online every week. She also occasionally holds forth on genre media on the *Dragoncon Classic Tracks Quarantime Panels*. She lives amid the spooky mountains of Southwest Virginia, right next to the Eastern Continental Divide.

**D.L. Cordero** is a fantasy author, occasional poet, and horror dabbler working out of Denver, CO. Their work can be found in several literary magazines and anthologies, such as *Prometheus Dreaming Magazine, Borderless Magazine, Listen To Your Skin: An Anthology of Queer and Self-Love*, and *Denver Noir* from

Akashic Books, which won the Colorado Book Award in 2023. They are also the voice of Cracogus in the audiodrama *Harbor*. In their advocacy work, Cordero has performed for institutions such as Denver Health Medical Center, Yale University, and The Transgender Center of the Rockies. When not storytelling, Cordero can be found wrangling their blind pitbull, thrifting for witchy oddities, and binging old-school anime. Follow them @dlcorderowrites and on dlcordero.com.

**Gia Kagan-Trenchard** is a writer, organizer, and attorney. Her writing has been featured on HBO's *Def Poetry*, TEDx, and at the Public Theater. Her play, *In Spite of Everything*, toured internationally as part of the Hip-Hop Theater Festival. Find her poetry book, *Murder Stay Murder*, from Penmanship Books. During the Trump Administration, Gia worked with the New Sanctuary Coalition, a multi-faith organization that supported undocumented immigrants. She's been an Adjunct Professor at New York Law School's Asylum Clinic. She also hosts a weekly creative writing workshop/support group for trauma workers, *These Rooms Don't Know Our Names*.

**David-Matthew Barnes** is the bestselling author of 16 novels, three collections of poetry, seven short stories, and more than 70 stage plays that have been performed in three languages in twelve countries. To date, he has written six produced screenplays. He writes in multiple genres, primarily young adult, romance, thriller, and horror. His literary work has appeared in over one hundred publications. He lives in Sacramento, California.

**LeAnne Hunt** (she/her) grew up in the Midwest and now lives in Orange County, California. She is a regular at the Two Idiots Peddling Poetry reading at the Ugly Mug in Orange. She has poems published in *Cultural Weekly, Spillway, Honey & Lime*, and *Lullaby of Teeth: An Anthology of Southern California Poets.* She publishes a blog of writing prompts and apologies at https://leannehunt.com/

**Sunni Jacocks (SJ)** (they/he) is a demi-demon boy with chaotic energy and has learned how to breathe with sunflowers growing within their chest. You can find more of his work in Sinclair Sexsmith's *The Best Lesbian Erotica of the Year, v. 7* and Rachel Kramer's *It Takes Two: Couples Erotica* anthology.

**Steve Ramirez** has never been captured on film (unless you count the spectral image taken at the 1951 séance). He keeps to himself at the wrong times. While attempting to dance with a drop of rain at the Enchantment Under the Sea dance in Wichita Falls, he discovered a talent for fog. Most nights, he can be found covering the pier. Yesterday morning, he accepted the award for Most Inspired before falling back asleep. Previous occupations include: coal miner, poltergeist, hubcap salesman, medical leech, spatial geographer, and mongoose.

**Alex B. Toklas** /@transboy_dreamer has only recently discovered how much he loves being in his body and is in a bit of a hurry to get that all sorted. His writing is forthcoming in *Deviant: Queer and Trans Desire* (Orlando Silver, ed.). He also writes under another name. Alex is a survivor. In his day job, his writing, and his everyday life, he works towards inclusive, trauma-aware, anti-racist, queer, and trans worldmaking. He isn't always on social media, but when he is, Alex likes to post kinky, trans smut.

**Lisbeth Coiman** is a warrior of internal battles and a trekker of intersecting paths in the route to becoming a world artist. Her debut book, *I Asked the Blue Heron: A Memoir* (2017), explores the intersection between immigration and mental health. Her poetry collection, *Uprising / Alzamiento* (Finishing Line Press, 2021) raises awareness of the humanitarian crisis in her homeland. Coiman lives in Los Angeles, CA where she hikes, dances salsa, and writes erotica for fun.

**Arwyn Carpenter** (they/them) is a queer, trans, nonbinary contemporary dancer and choreographer from Tkaronto, Canada. A member of the creative team for the Flight Festival of Contemporary Dance, which prioritizes presentation of Black and Indigenous dancers, Arwyn is interested in creating and facilitating decolonized art.

**Shari (share-ee) Caplan** (she/her) is the siren behind *Advice from a Siren* (Dancing Girl Press). Her poems have swum into *Gulf Coast, Painted Bride Quarterly, Angime, Drunk Monkeys, Luna Luna,* and elsewhere. Shari's work has earned her a scholarship to The Home School, a fellowship to The Vermont Studio Center, and nominations for a Bettering American Poetry Award and Pushcart Prize. She proudly serves as Madam Betty BOOM for The Poetry Brothel in Boston. Keep up with her at ShariCaplan.com

**Sinclair Sexsmith** (they/them) is a queer trans butch, a leather dominant, and a writer. They study dominance and submission, social & restorative justice, the energetic body, trauma, and transformation. Their short story collection, *Sweet & Rough: Queer Kink Erotica,* was a 2016 finalist for a Lambda Literary Award, and they have edited 5 editions of the *Best Lesbian Erotica* series, as well as the lesbian BDSM erotica anthology *Say Please, and Erotix: The Literary Journal of Somatics*. Since 2000, they have run the online erotica writing group Writing Spicy at writingspicy.com. Find Sinclair in all the places online at sugarbutch.net/find-sinclair.

**Byron F. Aspaas** was raised within the four sacred mountains of Dinétah. In a 2017 essay, "Nádleehí: One Who Changes," Aspaas explains how these elements are interconnected and under continuing threat. Aspaas's first published work was included in *Yellow Medicine Review* and since then his writing has appeared in numerous journals and anthologies. Aspaas's writing revisits the destruction of sacred land and engages his readers in a dialogue about preserving Diné culture and land. He uses imagery and persona to present explorations of language, landscape, and identity.

**Candice Reynolds** is a cisgender, lesbian, white, Canadian woman who writes sapphic romance and erotica. Newly wed to her wife E'Lece, Candice is brimming with romantic thoughts and feelings that she pours into her writing. Creating things for others to enjoy is one of the major passions of her life. Writing aside, Candice loves to cook and bake; she makes decorations from handmade paper flowers; she paints, and practices fibre arts of various kinds. Candice never grew out of the belief that dreams are wishes our hearts make, or that anything is possible if you believe. She cries a lot.

**Natalia J** is a singer/songwriter out of Boulder, Colorado. She loves writing poetry, and a lucky 10% of her poems evolve into songs. She writes to unveil her truth, to express her love for others, and to process the world around her.

**James Coats** is a multidisciplinary artist, author, and educator born in Los Angeles and raised in the Inland Empire. As a creative change agent, he believes the arts can inspire action and influence positive change in the world.

**Aiden Rondón** is a Venezuelan student who is currently trying to survive college and expects to become a translator, but his ambitions include literature and writing as well. They enjoy writing about horny elves, mages, and otherworldly beings in compromising circumstances whenever a good excuse arrives. He hopes to start posting about his cats, his little misfortunes and blessings, and other various things on his Instagram account, @antares.afterdark.whispers.

**Ben Trigg** dreams of being Truly Outrageous, striving to be a safe space for all, but especially the queer community. He is one third of Two Idiots Peddling Poetry at the Ugly Mug in Orange, California, a weekly series that has been running since 2000. Ben's poetry has been described (by him) as the sweet spot junction of heartfelt, pop culture, and comedy. His collection *Kindness from a Dark God* came out on Moon Tide Press in 2007. He co-edited the anthology *Don't Blame the Ugly Mug: 10 Years of 2 Idiots Peddling Poetry.* When all else fails, Ben goes to Disneyland.

**Geneviève** loves ukuleles, singing, the ocean, queer community, fucking the gender binary, casting spells for abundance and adventure, loving people in whatever ways feel right to those involved, extracting her thoughts/feels to alchemize into music and stories. She/ze is switchy as fuck and has a deep and abiding love for flogging people with roses, and teaches classes in it. Ze enjoys taking off her clothes for various reasons such as pleasure, money, and fun.

**Taneeka L. Wilder,** Bronx Native and self-published author of "On the Precipice of Love Illuminated," Taneeka L. Wilder uses her words to penetrate and nourish hearts for the purpose of healing, inspiration, and reflection. A multi-faceted creative, Taneeka has performed at numerous venues and featured on several platforms, including radio programs via Progressive Radio PRN.FM, *Live Hip-Hop Daily*, *The Author's Alley Show*, *The BOLD LIFE*, and *Midnight Meditations with Charlena*. Her work has also been featured in various anthologies through POETIX University, along with Elstabo, a literary compilation of sensual poetry. She has facilitated workshops on wellness, community building/healing, social justice, and is an avid dancer, music enthusiast, bibliophile, art and nature connoisseur. Her book is available on Amazon.

**Titus Androgynous** is a writer, multi-disciplinary performer, and drag king from Toronto, Canada. Their writing has appeared on stage, in *Xtra* and *Queeries* magazines, online at DapperQ.com, and most recently in *Best Lesbian Erotica of the Year*, Volume 6. Titus read their story, "The Kiss," at Listen to Your Skin in March 2022.

**Foxhaven** is the pseudonym of multi award-winning actor and playwright Margo MacDonald. Off-stage, her writing has appeared in *Ghosts of Ottawa* and *ARC Poetry Magazine*, as well as on HauntedWalk.com and SFSite.com. Her plays are usually about lost pieces of queer women's history and include *Shadows* (about lesbian theater maverick Eva Le Gallienne), *Maupin* (about the 17th century, cross-dressing, bisexual, swordfighter, opera singer, and duellist—Julie d'Aubigny Maupin), and *The Elephant Girls* (about an all-female gang in 1920s London). Margo lives in Toronto, Canada.

**Ellen Webre** is a biracial, Taiwanese-American poet, artist, and educator from Irvine, California. Her work has most recently been published in FreezeRay Press, *Sh!t Men Say to Me Anthology in Response to Toxic Masculinity, DARK INK: A Horror Anthology,* and *Voicemail Poems.* She is an avid supporter of the Southern Californian poetry community, currently acting as a social media marketing specialist and videographer for Moon Tide Press and Two Idiots Peddling Poetry.

**Beaux Neal** is a poet, musician, dancer, and more. She was born and raised in Atlanta, GA, where she currently lives, works, writes, and dreams. Her work, which often swings towards the dark and emotionally macabre, has been featured in *Black Telephone Magazine* (an imprint of Clash Books), Metatron Press, Dream Boy Book Club, and more. Both of her bands start with the letter L, and you can find all of the dirt @hannahbolecter on Instagram.

**Leah Rogin** wants to reintroduce the world to Marilyn Monroe as a radical, bisexual, intellectual. Leah also writes about birds, water, and time. She lives in the mountains west of Denver.

**Sarah LaRue** (she/her) is a health advocate, activist, and a queer jewish witch poet. She moved to Denver after living in DC, Boston, and PDX. Sarah has been published in *Stain'd Arts* and The Opiate publications, and her work has been featured by the University of Washington Whiteley Center. Her two self-published books, and information about her acupuncture practice, are available at hybridhealing.co. Sarah loves quiet nights and her ancient kitten Banzai.

**Cleo Black** spent her life identifying as a reader of all things, an inquisitive soul who wants to be in school, in libraries, in museums. Of course, she has always been a poet and a writer, too, but is just starting to admit it to herself by devoting time to the craft. She believes that we need community to heal trauma, that articulating our experiences and practicing deep listening bonds us. We are all teachers. We are all students. Our purpose is to explore and expand love.

**Oliver Antoni Krawczyk** is a poet situated in Milwaukee, WI. He is the guest judge for Table//Feast's Kenan Ince award and has been published in the *West Review, The Wisconsin Historical Society Press, One Art,* and elsewhere online and in print. He's taught formal poetry classes through Gris Literatura. When not writing, he can be found playing with makeup and belting out showtunes at karaoke.

**Emily Marie Passos Duffy** is a poet, performing artist, and author of *Hemorrhaging Want & Water* (Perennial Press 2023). She was a finalist for the Noemi Press 2020 Book Award and a finalist of the 2020 Inverted Syntax Sublingua Prize for Poetry. She was named a 2020 Disquiet International Luso-American fellow. She received her MFA from the Jack Kerouac School of Disembodied Poetics at Naropa University in 2018. Currently, she is writing, researching, and enjoying sips of espresso at all times of the day in Lisbon, where she lives with her orange cat, Magda.

**Orlando Silver** (he/they) is a performer and writer from Sydney, Australia. He is the author of *Soft Fruit* (2022), *Relent* (2023), and the editor of *I Write the Body* (2023) published by Kith Books. He can be found here: orlandosilver.substack.com/

**Kat Sanford** is a polyamorous and chaotic neutral bisexual MILF. On weekdays, she runs a small bookkeeping firm out of her living room, and the rest of the time she spends watching various inane children's shows and talking about poop with her 6-year-old twins. She spent many years writing and editing and coaching poetry slams, but more recently enjoys small group writing workshops with no competitive agenda. She thinks you're beautiful and would love to chat with you over coffee.

**Liv Mammone** (she/her) is an editor and poet from Long Island, New York. Her poetry has appeared in *wordgathering*, *Monstering Magazine*, *Wicked Banshee*, *The Medical Journal of Australia*, and others. In 2017, she competed for Union Square Slam as the first disabled woman to be on a New York national poetry slam team. She was also a finalist in the Capturing Fire National Poetry Slam in 2017. She has edited multiple books across genres including the *Margins and Murmerations* novels by trans activist Otter Lieffe, and the poetry collection *They Called Her Goddess We Named her Girl* by Uma Dwivedi, which was nominated for a Write Bloody Book Award. A Brooklyn Poets Fellow and Zoeglossia fellow, she works currently as an editor at Game Over Books. In 2022, she was one of the top 10 most read poets in the *Split this Rock* database (*The Quarry*).

**Jessica Lawson** (she/her/hers) is Denver-based writer, teacher, and queer single parent. Her debut book of poetry, *Gash Atlas* (2022), was selected by judge Erica Hunt for the Kore Press Institute Poetry Prize, and her chapbook *Rot Contracts* was published in 2020 (Trouble Department). Of *Gash Atlas,* Joyelle McSweeney writes, "Jessica Lawson turns the log-book of patriarchy inside out." A Pushcart-nominated poet, Lawson's work has appeared in *The Rumpus; Entropy; ANMLY; Dreginald; Yes, Poetry; The Wanderer; Cosmonauts Avenue*; and elsewhere.

**Stina French** is an ex-professor and Headmistress of The Sexploratorium, a center for adult sex education. Her work has appeared in *Manifest Station, Heavy Feather Review, Grimoire, Sh!t Men Say to Me Anthology in Response to Toxic Masculinity*, among others. She wears welts from the Bible Belt and hosts Listen To Your Skin reading series. Find it on Facebook or IG @listen2yourskin. She has edited two anthologies, this one and one on religious trauma called *Take The Fruit*.

**Aerik Francis** is a Queer Black and Latinx poet and teaching artist based in Denver. They're a Canto Mundo poetry fellow and a The Watering Hole fellow, as well as a poetry reader for *Underblong* and a coordinator/host of Slam Nuba. Aerik recently released an EP of poetry-songs called *SYZYGY* (find on Bandcamp) and has a chapbook titled *BODYELECTRONIC* coming in April '22 from Trouble Department Press. Find their published poetry at phaentompoet.com. Find them on IG/TW/youtube/soundcloud @phaentompoet.

**ellie swensson** is a southern queer femme living in Athens, GA. she is currently reimagining her creative practice and working as a community engagement and culture planner for the Atlanta region. she holds an MFA in Writing & Poetics from Naropa University (2015) and a Masters in Urban Panning and Design from UGA (2023). she is the founder/co-director of Writers Warehouse. swensson is a community builder who believes that poetics is what occurs where eros, divinity, activism, and careful craft intersect. her poems are published in a handful of places you may know, but she prefers her words alive in the mouth and the body. *salt of us,* her debut full length poetry collection, was published in 2019.

*9798218372262*
WS - #0058 - 240125 - C0 - 229/152/12 - PB - 9798218372262 - Gloss Lamination